D1096920

When There Is Love

The McKinleys
Book 3

Kimberly Rae Jordan

THREE**STRAND**
P R E S S

A CORD OF THREE STRANDS IS NOT EASILY BROKEN.

A man, a woman & their God.

Three Strand Press publishes Christian Romance stories

that intertwine love, faith and family.

Always clean. Always heartwarming. Always uplifting.

CHAPTER ONE

VICTORIA McKinley slumped back against her chair and scowled at the error screen on her monitor. "No. Please..."

She squeezed her eyes shut and said a quick prayer before opening them again, hoping against hope that the error message would have magically disappeared. But no such luck. It had been happening more and more frequently, and once again, all the data she'd entered—and not saved—was gone.

Her gaze went to where her cell phone sat beside the keyboard. She had been putting it off for weeks, but in the past few days, on top of the error messages and system shutdowns she'd been getting, the tower had begun to make a horrible sound. She simply couldn't afford to lose everything that was on the computer.

The only choice left to her was to call the person who'd set it up in the first place. The one who had threatened her with all sorts of dire consequences if she ever dared take it to anyone but him for servicing.

Trent Hause.

If she hadn't been so worried about losing all her data, she would have happily defied him and gone to some random computer place. But in addition to that, carting the tower anyplace was pretty much impossible for her. She'd have had to call her dad or Eric and then they'd want to know why she didn't ask Trent to help. After all, he took care of all the computer issues in their family.

With a sigh, Victoria reached out and picked up her phone. After the briefest of hesitations, she tapped on Trent's contact information then put it on speakerphone. It rang three times, and she was just about ready to hang up when the call went through.

"Hang on. I need to look out the window."

Frowning, Victoria looked down at the phone. Had she called the wrong person? It sure *sounded* like Trent's voice. "What?"

"To see if pigs are flying. Fortunately, I cannot confirm that hell has frozen over, but I figure pigs flying would be easy enough to see."

Victoria couldn't keep the corners of her mouth from turning up in a smile. "Pigs are not flying."

"Then why are you calling? I'm pretty sure that was the requirement that had to be met before you'd call me."

"Yes. I know." Victoria sighed. "Unfortunately, I'm in dire straits here, and you're the only one that can help me."

"Really now?" Trent dragged the words out. "Those are words I never thought I'd hear from Miss Victoria McKinley."

"I suppose I could take my problem to Drake's Fast Computer Repair Shop down the street."

"Oh no, you don't."

Victoria could almost picture him sitting straight up in his chair. "So you'll help me?"

"Of course, I'll help you, babe. I have a meeting this afternoon but should be done by five. I can stop by your place afterward. Would that be okay?"

"Yes, that would be fine." She paused. "Thank you, Trent."

"You're very welcome."

Silence stretched between them before Victoria said, "Well, I'll let you get back to work."

"Yep. See you in a few hours."

After she hung up, Victoria gave one last withering glare at her computer before sliding off the chair and heading for the kitchen. She mentally flipped through the contents of her fridge and cupboards to see what she could pull together for a meal. It might not be the wisest decision, but if the man was going to come fix her computer, the least she could do was provide him with dinner.

Thankfully, she'd gone shopping with her mom earlier in the week. It was a chore she disliked, but her mom always turned it into a girls' day out with lunch included so it was a little more tolerable. Victoria hated that she had to rely on her mom to help her, but there was just no way to reach a lot of the stuff on the grocery shelves by herself. That left her with two alternatives: ask someone for help or let her mom come along. Since she hated the thought of asking random strangers for help, the choice really was a no-brainer.

Victoria slipped her arms into the cuffs of her crutches and gripped the handles. She tried not to think about how often she needed to use the walking aides lately. Though she still didn't need them all the time, she knew that point was coming sooner rather than later. Once that happened, her family would know just how much pain her hip caused her. Hoping to keep that knowledge from them as long as she could, she used the crutches whenever she was alone. Too bad it wasn't a permanent solution.

She walked into the kitchen and climbed up on the stool she kept there to see what was in her freezer. Though fridges with freezers on the bottom had gained popularity in recent years, hers was still the older style since she needed access to the freezer portion less frequently.

With a package of frozen chicken breasts in her hand, she climbed down to put it on the counter. It would be nice to cook a meal for more than just one. Even though she lived on her own, Victoria still took the time to cook for herself since cooking was something she enjoyed doing. Her mother had made certain that both she and her older sister Brooke had learned to bake and cook at a young age.

Now that her plan for the afternoon had been squashed, she had time to prepare a meal. It wasn't a big sacrifice to put off doing the paperwork for her business—The Accessibility Solutions Company—since it was her least favorite part of the job, but because of the computer issues, she'd been putting it off a bit too frequently of late. Hopefully, Trent would be able to fix it quickly so she could keep from getting too much further behind.

It was just after five thirty when Trent pulled his Jeep to a stop behind Victoria's car in her driveway. He still couldn't believe she'd actually called him, even if it was for a computer issue. No doubt she'd debated going against what he'd asked of her when he'd set up her system—that she wouldn't go anywhere but him for repairs.

He grabbed the plastic bag from the seat next to him and then got his laptop bag from the backseat. As he walked along the sidewalk that led to the covered porch, Trent noticed the bright flowers planted in the beds in front of the house. The small front yard was immaculately landscaped, and he would bet dollars to donuts that Victoria took care of it all.

That woman didn't let anything stop her from doing what needed to be done. It was one of the many things he admired about her.

He pushed the doorbell and looked around as he waited for her to answer the door. She'd chosen a quaint little neighborhood to live in. It was definitely a world away from the somewhat sterile apartment he called home these days. Truth was, he hesitated to buy a house for himself just yet because he hoped to share a home with a wife one day and wanted it to be something she would like, too. Or, alternatively, if she already owned her own place, he could just move in with her. After getting married, of course.

When he heard the door open, Trent swung back around, a ready smile on his face.

"Hey, Victoria."

"Hi, Trent. C'mon in." She moved back and once he'd stepped into the house, she closed the door behind him.

His stomach rumbled at the wonderful smells permeating the air. A clear reminder that the sandwich he'd had for lunch had been hours ago.

"Here. I got this for you." Trent reached into the plastic bag and pulled out an ice cold bottle of the specialized water he'd seen Victoria drink on more than one occasion. He'd stopped at the convenience store just down the block from her house and bought cold drinks for both of them.

"Thanks." She smiled as she took it from him. "How did you know I like to drink this stuff?"

Trent shrugged. "I've seen you with it a few times."

"You're one of those observant kind of guys, huh?"

"About some things," Trent replied, although in truth—given his job with BlackThorpe—he was pretty observant about everything. It was something Marcus Black and Alex Thorpe drilled into them on a regular basis.

Be alert. Be aware.

"Well, come observe what my computer's doing and tell me it's not at death's door."

As he followed her into the living room where her computer was set up, Trent noticed that she wore a white denim skirt and turquoise T-shirt. Her hair was gathered into a ponytail that swept back and forth across her shoulders as she walked. She seemed to be favoring her left leg, but he couldn't be completely sure. He wasn't often in the position of watching her walk like this, so perhaps that was her normal gait.

"That's what popped up," Victoria said as they reached the computer desk.

The message on the monitor drew his attention from Victoria. He frowned as he read it, settling into the chair she'd turned toward him. "Is this the first time you've seen it?"

"No. It's shown up a few times."

A sudden rattling sound came from the tower at his feet. "And how long has it been doing that?"

"About a week?"

He glanced over and saw she was standing at the corner of the desk, a sheepish look on her face. With him seated, they were almost at eye level with each other. Her chocolate brown gaze met his. He lifted his eyebrows at her response.

"Okay. It's been about two weeks since it first started making that sound."

"And the messages?" he asked with a jerk of his head in the direction of the monitor.

She bit her lip for a second and then said, "I've been getting them off and on for about a month or so."

"A *month or so*, Victoria?" Trent sighed, looking down at the tower as it gave a particularly loud rattle. "Why didn't you call me sooner?" When she didn't answer right away, he lifted his gaze to find her watching him, one eyebrow quirked. "Yeah. Never mind."

He turned his attention back to the computer. So he'd maybe been coming on a little strong with his flirting lately. It was a bit disheartening to realize that she'd only contacted him out of sheer desperation. She'd put off calling him for over a month at the risk of losing her business and personal records.

Well, he'd do what he could to get her back on track computer-wise and then he'd need to rethink his approach to things. Though they'd only met because of Eric, he'd liked her almost from the start. At first, she'd been a curiosity for him. He'd never been around someone with dwarfism before, so their initial interactions had more to do with him wanting to learn more about her as a little person. Slowly, they'd become friends of a sort, and he'd enjoyed spending time with her and the rest of the McKinleys when he could.

It wasn't until earlier that year that things had kind of changed for him. Quite out of the blue he'd realized he was accepting Eric's invitations in hopes of being able to spend time with Victoria. And the disappointment he'd experienced if it turned out that she wasn't there was far more than it should be for just a friend. A few months ago, he'd begun to test the waters to see if she might be interested in him as well. He'd been wary of facing it head on since he realized it might take Victoria a little bit longer to get used to the idea, not just because he was her brother's best friend, but also because he was of average-size.

Unfortunately, his lighthearted attempts at flirting hadn't had their intended effect. It seemed she'd never viewed him as more than a friend and now even their friendship—such as it was—had been strained because of how he felt about her. He hoped it wasn't too late to get back to that friendship, because this whole computer situation brought home to him how truly uncomfortable she was with his attempts to take things to the next level.

"This is going to take me a little while. If you have plans, I can work on it at my place," Trent said as he tapped some keys to get rid of the error screen.

"I have no plans, but if you do, feel free to take it with you and work on it when you have the time."

"Since my best friend up and got married, my Friday night and weekend social life has dropped drastically. I had no plans that my DVR can't take care of."

"Well, in that case, I made some supper if you're hungry."

Surprised, Trent glanced at her. "Uh, sure. It smells delicious."

"It's nothing too fancy."

"And what about me makes you think I only eat fancy food?" Trent asked as he turned his attention back to the computer. "Let me just get this set to back up the hard drive and then we can eat while it does that."

"Sounds good. I'll just go finish it up."

Trent resisted the urge to turn and watch her walk to the kitchen. Instead, he groaned when he saw how long it had been since a backup had been run on the system. He was going to have to teach her a few more things this time around.

He used his own credit card to purchase a backup program for her. It took a few minutes to get it all set up, but soon the program was backing up her system online. At least this way, if the machine took a dump, her work files were protected.

Knowing the backup would take a while, Trent pushed back from the desk and went to the kitchen. As he took in the round table that was set for them, his gut clenched. His resolve to keep things friendly threatened to crumble around him. This setting came way too close to resembling the intimate dinners for two he'd pictured over the past few months.

"What would you like to drink?"

He looked to where Victoria stood behind the counter, obviously on a stool of some sort. She dropped the cucumbers she'd just finished slicing into the bowl of salad in front of her. With quick movements, she mixed it all together.

"Water is fine."

"Can you just grab the glasses from the table and fill them there, please?" She tilted her head toward the fridge.

With a nod, Trent grabbed the two glasses and went to the water dispenser on the front of the fridge to fill them. Pushing one glass against the dispenser, he watched over his shoulder as Victoria climbed down the stool and reached for the salad bowl. She put it on the table then returned to the kitchen. She grabbed the stool by its upright handle and moved it to the stove.

He returned both glasses to the table. "Is there anything else you need me to do?"

Victoria glanced at him then back to the stove as if debating. "Actually, if you'd drain the vegetables for me, that would be great."

Happy that she'd accepted his offer of help, Trent joined her at the stove. She still stood on her stool which brought the top of her head to his shoulder. When she glanced up at him, it seemed that she realized how close they were, too, as her brown eyes widened briefly.

CHAPTER TWO

THE, uh, strainer is in the sink." Victoria turned the handle of the pot so it was facing him.

As Trent reached for it, she climbed off the stool and moved it back to the counter. Once he'd taken the pot from the stove and stepped in front of the sink to empty it into the strainer, she opened the oven. The delicious aromas he'd smelled when he walked in the door earlier intensified.

Trent was concerned about her burning herself, but she proved to be quite adept as she removed a casserole dish from the oven and climbed the stool to put it on the potholders on the counter. He could only imagine how inconvenient it must be for her to have to constantly climb up and down that stool in order to function in her own kitchen. And yet she made it look easy, and she did it without complaint.

She held out a bowl to him. "You can put the vegetables in that."

He did as she requested and then put the bowl on the table. "Want me to put that on the table, too?"

"Sure." She pushed the rectangular dish across the counter to him. "I'll just get the potatoes, and we can eat."

Swallowing past the tightness in his throat, Trent wished he could rewind time. He'd tell her to take her computer to another person. Anyone but him. This was just too much. It was giving him a taste of something he'd only dreamed of up to that point. Even before he'd met Victoria, he'd eaten many lonely meals wishing—hoping—for something just like this.

"Have a seat," Victoria said. After she had slid the bowl with the potatoes onto the table, she stood staring for a moment. "I guess that's all."

Trent would have liked to be the gentleman and help Victoria with her seat, but since she'd already directed him to sit down, he settled into the chair she'd indicated.

When she sat down across from him, she said, "Would you like to pray?"

He nodded and bowed his head to say grace, certain that any moment he'd wake up to find this was all just another one of the dreams he'd had over the years. He knew it was one of the reasons he enjoyed being with the McKinleys so much. They had welcomed him without reserve and given him a taste of a dream they'd never known he'd had. To be part of a family who loved and cared about each other.

"So, how did you end up being such a whiz at computers?" Victoria asked after he'd finished praying.

As he took the bowl of salad she handed him, Trent said, "Well, it all started with a nerdy teenager whose parents gave him pretty much anything he asked for."

Victoria slid a piece of chicken onto her plate then looked up at him. "Your parents spoiled you?"

"Not so much spoiled. I was their third child. An oopsie baby, apparently. My brother was ten and my sister seven when I was born. My parents didn't really have room for a baby in their lives by that point, but they had plenty of money so they hired a nanny to take care of me. By the time I was a teenager, as long as I didn't cause trouble, they would give me whatever I asked for." He smiled at the memory. "I asked for lots of very expensive computers and accessories."

"That's kind of like me with Eric and Brooke. Except for the nanny part." She grinned "And the lots of money."

"Yes, you were fortunate." Trent cut his chicken, not sure he should have revealed all of that to Victoria, but it had seemed right to tell her.

She nodded. "So you spent most your time on your computers?"

"Yes. I got bullied in school, so my computers were a safe place for me."

"Bullied? For what?"

Trent debated telling her about his experiences. They wouldn't come close to what she'd likely suffered over the years, but she *had* asked. "I was a scrawny teenager. I never really hit the growth spurt that all my peers did in high school. I've always been smaller than most guys."

Victoria tilted her head. "You're not small."

He smiled at her. "I realize that from your perspective that's probably how it appears, but from mine, it's a bit different. I'm usually a good four to six inches shorter than most the guys I hang out with. Take Eric, for example. Dude is over six feet while I'm closer to five-nine."

"Well, you definitely don't seem to be scrawny anymore, even if you are a bit shorter than other guys."

It pleased him that she'd noticed he worked out. He didn't really have a choice at BlackThorpe. Not that he wouldn't have done it on his own anyway, but working for that company had made it necessary. "I can hold my own now but I couldn't back then. And though I wasn't into sports or anything, I had my own way of leveling the playing field."

Victoria's brows drew together. "What did you do?"

"Nothing I'm proud of, to be honest, but those years in high school laid the groundwork for my job at BlackThorpe, so I don't completely regret them."

She stared at him for a moment then her eyes widened. "You were a hacker."

The only people who knew the extent of his background worked at BlackThorpe. "Eric tell you that?"

"No. It makes sense though." She took a sip of water, curiosity in her eyes.

"Yeah, it does. But like I said, I'm not proud of some of the stuff I did. I was lucky that I didn't get caught before I got my act together and realized that what I was doing was wrong."

"God had a plan for you."

Trent nodded, grateful for the housekeeper and her husband who had taken an interest in his spiritual life during his teens. They had also given him a glimpse of what a loving family looked like. It had been enough to stir the desire for one deep within him. "Yes, He did. He does still."

They continued to talk about his computer experiences as they ate. Right then, there was no other way that Trent would have wanted to spend his Friday evening. A delicious meal. Victoria actually talking with him. It was as close to perfect as possible.

"I have some dessert, but I thought maybe we could have it a little later if you needed to do something on the computer."

Trent nodded. "I'll go check on it. I'm doing a backup of your hard drive so if it fails, you won't lose everything."

"Thank you." She gave him a sheepish smile. "I guess I should have called you sooner."

"Or even just mentioned it to me when you saw me any number of times over the past few weeks," he said with a wink. "It's not like we haven't been in the same place multiple times."

Victoria sat back in her chair and sighed. "Okay, I think it's been well-established that I was a fool for not asking for help sooner."

"I'll let it slide this time since you fed me such a wonderful dinner, but next time as soon as something strange pops up or sounds funny, you let me know." He gave her a firm look. "Promise?"

Victoria raised a hand. "I promise."

"Good." Trent pushed back from the table. "Now, let me help you clear this up."

"Don't worry about that," Victoria said as she slid off her chair. "I've got it under control."

Ignoring her dismissal of his offer to help, Trent picked up the heavier of the dishes and set them on the counter and then stacked their plates beside them. "I'll let you handle them from here."

"Thank you." She didn't sound particularly grateful, no doubt put out because he'd overridden her assurance that she had it under control.

Trent didn't care. She probably assumed it had to do with her size and the added challenge of moving around and climbing up and down the stool. But honestly, he would have done it for any woman who'd gone to the trouble of cooking him dinner. Knowing that his actions would make things easier for her, just made it that much sweeter.

She remained stubbornly silent as she worked on cleaning up the kitchen as Trent returned to the computer to check on its status. He breathed a sigh of relief when he saw that it backed everything up successfully. At least now her business records were no longer at risk.

Too bad he was still going to have to give her some bad news.

Victoria took her time putting away the food and loading the dishwasher. She knew she should have been more accepting of Trent's help, but it was so engrained in her to do it herself when she could. It was enough that she had to rely on his help with her computer. Clearing the table was something she could handle, and he was already doing so much for her.

But if she was honest with herself, she was actually grateful for his help. In spite of her claims to the contrary, Victoria knew she couldn't handle it all anymore. The reality—which she was still loathe to accept—was that over the course of the past several months, her left hip had begun to give her more trouble. In fact, there was rarely a day without pain anymore. Climbing up and down the stool so often like she had done today was something she would likely pay for before the night was over. But she was glad to have done it for Trent. It was the least she could do since he was helping her out.

She glanced to where Trent sat with his back to her at the computer, his broad shoulders hunched forward as he stared at the monitor. During their dinner, she'd learned more about him than she'd known over the almost three years since they'd first met. He'd always been Eric's best friend, so they hadn't really spent any time together by themselves and certainly hadn't held any in-depth conversations with each other.

Oh, they'd joked and talked some over the years when he'd tagged along with Eric to family or church functions. She had counted him a friend—not a close one—but a friend nonetheless. Until things had started to change back in January. Suddenly, he was showing up at her doorstep to shovel her snow. And his lighthearted conversations with her started to have a more flirtatious undertone to them. She'd tried to just brush it aside, but there had been a small part of her that had liked it. A little too much. That had been enough to get her to back right off from everything with him.

Slowly, Victoria climbed the stool again and reached for the covered pan on the counter. She pulled the lid off the pan to reveal the chocolate cake she'd made earlier. From previous experience, she was fairly certain it was a dessert he'd like. She just hoped he realized she'd done all this as a way of thanking him for his help...nothing more.

She was cutting the cake when he got up from the desk and came to the counter. Using a spatula, she lifted a piece of cake from the pan onto the plate she'd set out.

"That looks delicious," Trent said as he leaned against the counter. "Did you make it from scratch?"

"Of course." She set a fork on the plate and slid it across to him. "According to my mother, that's the only way to do it."

"Well, your mother has certainly taught you well."

Victoria gave him a quick smile. Caroline McKinley prided herself on having made sure that her daughters were both well-versed in cooking, baking and running a home. And Victoria hadn't been given any special dispensation because of her dwarfism. Her mother had just worked harder to find ways for her to do anything that presented a challenge.

"There's ice cream in the freezer if you'd like some." Victoria put another piece on the remaining plate. "Do you want coffee?"

Trent shook his head. "This is just fine."

Victoria stepped down off the stool and reached for her plate only to find that Trent had already picked it up and was carrying both his and hers to the table. With a sigh, she rounded the counter and sat back down across from him. "So what's the verdict on my machine?"

Trent swallowed the bite he'd just taken. "Good news is that I managed to get all your files backed up online, so there're no worries about you losing data at this point."

"Thank you. That's a relief. I've lost a bit of work over the past month when it's had that error occur."

Trent gave her an exasperated look as he took another bite of the cake. "Well, that's where the bad news comes in."

"Bad news?" Victoria sat back in her chair. "What's the bad news?"

"You need a new system."

"A new system? Is this one really that far gone?"

"Yes and honestly, it's just simply out of date. Computer technology changes quickly, and you've had this system for almost three years now, right?"

Victoria nodded. He had set it up for her not long after they had first met.

"You won't have to spend a lot of money to get a system much superior to the one you have. This time I'm going to set it up a bit better than I did before. And train you more on it."

Victoria looked over to where her computer sat. "How much will a new system cost me?"

"I don't know exactly because I'm going to build it myself. That way I can customize it for you."

"You don't have to do that. I'm sure you've got better things to do."

Trent shrugged. "Not really. Like I said...best friend gets married and social life takes a nose dive."

"If you're sure..."

"I am. Maybe as payment for my services you could make me another meal sometime."

Victoria chuckled. "I guess we each have things we do well."

"And you do yours exceptionally well," Trent said then put the last bite of cake into his mouth.

His praise brought warmth to her cheeks. Before she could say anything, Trent's phone rang. He pulled it from the holder on his belt and looked at the display before putting it to his ear.

"What's up?"

Victoria concentrated on the last few bites of her cake while he listened to whoever was on the other end of the call.

"Actually, I'm at your sister's at the moment."

She jerked her head up and gave it a shake.

"Uh, no. I'm not at Brooke's. Victoria was having some computer problems and contacted me to see if I could help her out."

Victoria groaned. There was a reason she'd gone directly to Trent instead of contacting Eric first. She'd known that in the end, Eric would have sent Trent her way, so she'd decided to just skip that step in hopes of avoiding any rumors. But now...

"Yeah. Her system is kinda toast, so I'm going to build her a new one."

After she had finished her cake, Victoria took both plates into the kitchen. She had thought about offering him a second piece but after he'd told Eric he was with her, he'd forfeited that privilege.

"I'll ask her and let you know," Trent said before ending the call.

"What's up with Eric?"

"He said he tried to call you. Is something wrong with your phone?"

Victoria reached for the cell phone where it sat on the counter and checked the screen. "Nope. Just dead." With a sigh, she plugged it in and set it down on the counter to charge.

"Well, apparently your mom agreed to take Sarah for an overnight, so Eric wondered if we wanted to go to a movie with them. Alicia is going as well as Brooke and Lucas."

Truthfully, she was tired and sore and didn't really want to go out, but she also didn't want to have to explain why she was declining the invitation.

Trent must have seen from her expression that she was toying with the idea of not going because he said, "What if I promise no flirting tonight? Just friends hanging out together. It won't be anything like a date."

"Really?" Victoria laced the word heavily with doubt even though that hadn't been the primary reason for her hesitancy.

"Really," Trent said with a nod, his expression serious. "I won't even offer you a ride."

Well, that was unfortunate because she probably would have taken him up on that offer.

"However, if you'd like a ride, I would gladly give you one."

Victoria looked at him again, trying to gauge his seriousness. His blue eyes didn't move as he held her gaze, but she couldn't read anything else in his expression. She couldn't help but wonder what was behind the sudden shift in his attitude toward her. As recent as the previous weekend, he'd still been giving outlandish suggestions for where they could go for their first date. Had seeing her in her own environment dealing with all the things she dealt with as a little person changed how he viewed her? She wouldn't have been surprised. Only another person with dwarfism could truly understand the challenges she faced on a daily basis.

Other than her family, most people—while admiring how she got along—weren't really interested in the reality of *how* she managed to do it. Though Trent had been a part of her world these past three years, it had really been on the periphery. His coming to her home had drawn him from the edges of her life into more of her day to day reality. Even so, he still didn't know it all. And if what he'd seen that evening had been enough to make him back off, a full dose of her life would have sent him running.

"Okay. I'll go. And I will take you up on that ride if you don't mind. I can probably get a ride home with Alicia afterward."

"Whatever works for you." He turned toward the computer. "Although, if it would be okay with you, I'd rather leave my laptop bag here. I'll pick it up when I drop you off. I don't really want to leave it in the Jeep since it's a work laptop."

"That's fine." She glanced down at herself. "Let me just freshen up. I'll be right back."

CHAPTER THREE

In the bathroom off her bedroom, Victoria pulled the elastic from her ponytail so that her hair hung down past her shoulders. She gave it a quick brush through before adding a sweep of gloss to her lips. Staring into the mirror, she caught glimpses of both Brooke and her half-sister, Alicia, in her reflection. She didn't have the facial features associated with the most common type of dwarfism since hers was caused by a different gene mutation. Anyone seeing her from the shoulders up wouldn't know that she was a little person, but since she was more than just her face, their attention usually focused on the parts that *did* reveal her dwarfism.

Pushing aside the feelings that came from that thought, Victoria turned away from the mirror and made use of the facilities since she didn't relish having to go the public washrooms at the theater. Once she was all done in the bathroom, she returned to the living room to find Trent standing at the big bay window gazing out at the street.

"Ready to go?" she asked as she picked up her purse from the coffee table.

Trent turned from the window and smiled, his whole face lighting up. Her heart skipped a beat. When his easy and frequent smiles were directed specifically at her, she had a hard time not reacting. They almost made her reconsider her decision to keep her distance from him romantically.

Though her phone still didn't have much of a charge, she went ahead and slipped it into her purse before heading for the door. He followed her out of the house and then went to his car while she locked up. As she approached the shiny vehicle sitting in her driveway, Victoria hoped that she'd be able to get in with little hassle. She was grateful that, for whatever reason, Trent had chosen not to drive a big truck.

He opened the door for her as she approached. "Will you be able to get in?"

She probably could but rather than take the chance, Victoria dug her keys from her purse and pressed the fob to open the trunk of her car. "I'll just get the stool I keep in my trunk."

"I'll do it."

As she watched Trent lift the stool from the trunk, Victoria was grateful he hadn't offered to pick her up and put her on the seat. So far, they'd had no physical contact that went further than what she had with her other male friends. Him picking her up would have moved them into an area she wasn't sure she'd be comfortable with.

"Here you go." Trent placed the stool on the driveway between the door and the vehicle.

She was able to climb the steps of the stool and settle herself on the seat with little effort. "Thank you. Sorry for the hassle."

"Wasn't a problem, babe." He flashed her a quick smile that crinkled the skin at the corners of his eyes, then shut the door for her.

She heard the door behind her open and then close and assumed he'd put the stool in since they were going to need it again. It took her a couple of tries to get the seatbelt fastened correctly because her hands weren't quite steady, and she wasn't sure why. He'd promised not to flirt, but for some reason she was more nervous than ever around him. Taking her own car would definitely have been the better idea, but the thought of driving with the way her hip had been aching had not been appealing. However, she wasn't sure that her current predicament was actually the lesser of two evils.

"So when you guys go to the movies en mass, what sort of flick do you usually end up seeing? Given that you girls outnumber us guys, I'm not holding out much hope for the latest action adventure."

Victoria chuckled. "Actually, that's where you'd be wrong. Brooke and I tend to side with Eric when it comes to the type of movie we want to watch. Staci and Alicia try for the chick flick or romantic comedy movies, but we usually end up with something more sci-fi or action oriented. Of course, Staci has a little more sway over Eric these days."

"What about Lucas?" Trent asked as he pulled out onto the main road in the direction of the shopping mall where the theater was located.

"Haven't gone to too many movies with him yet, but from what I'm seen, as long as Brooke's happy, so is he."

"Smart man," Trent observed. "So basically it could go either way tonight."

"You might be the tie breaker," Victoria told him.

He slowed to a stop at a red light. "And if I decide I'm in the romantic comedy mood?"

Victoria laughed. "Well, I hope the meal I just prepared you turns sour in your stomach, and you have to spend the whole time in the bathroom."

Trent grinned at her. "Action adventure it is."

Victoria's phone chirped, and she dug it out of her purse to look at the display. "Eric says they're already there." The phone went again. "And he's giving us two choices for movies."

"Well, toss my vote in with whatever you want to see." The vehicle surged forward as the light turned green. "Unless you're pulling my leg about what movies you actually do like to see."

"Not to worry. Neither movie is a chick flick or a romance." She told him the titles, and they discussed what they'd heard about each film for the rest of the drive. Once they pulled up in front of the theater, they'd agreed on the movie they would be voting to see.

"Do you want me to let you off at the door?" Trent asked.

Victoria hesitated but then shook her head. "I'm fine to walk."

He found a spot that was relatively close, so once she used the stool to get out of the Jeep, they didn't have to walk too far. As usual, Victoria was aware of the looks she got as they made their way to the stairs that led up to the theater doors. She didn't mind the curious stares of children who didn't seem to know what to make of someone who was their size but looked like an adult. She was less forgiving of adults who were rude enough to openly stare or make comments like she was deaf instead of just short.

Trent opened one of the glass doors and held it for her.

"Thank you," she said as she walked past him.

Almost immediately, she spotted Eric and Staci where they stood together off to the side. Her sister-in-law was leaning against Eric as his hand rubbed up and down her back. Victoria felt an unusual rush of jealousy as she watched them. Though Staci was beautiful with her long blonde hair and fine features, Victoria knew that her brother's love and adoration of his wife had little to do with how she looked. They made a striking couple where they stood, drawing the gazes of people passing them by. Kind of like with her and Trent, except in Eric and Staci's case it was because of the attractive picture they made, not like the odd one Victoria and Trent presented.

Staci straightened as they neared and smiled. "Glad you could make it, Tori."

"Thanks. I'm surprised you guys decided to spend your kid-free evening with us."

"Well, we won't be with you all night," Eric said with a grin.

Before either she or Trent could reply, Alicia joined them followed a few minutes later by Brooke and Lucas. As Victoria watched her sister walk toward them hand in hand with Lucas, she was still amazed that any man had managed to break through the wall around Brooke's heart. She was grateful that not only had Lucas brought love to Brooke's life, he'd brought a softening to her heart that had helped to heal the hurts that had lasted far too long within their family.

As she watched Brooke smile with affection at Eric and Staci, Victoria felt a shaft of pain at the reminder that even though they were sisters, they still weren't that close. What Brooke hadn't known—and never would—was that some of what she'd shared after making things right with her dad had hurt Victoria deeply. She had listened with a growing ache in her heart as Brooke had talked about how much she'd hurt when they'd had to leave the two orphan children they'd been fostering in Africa. Victoria's pain had come from knowing that Brooke had cared more about those two baby girls than she had her own sister. For whatever reason, Brooke hadn't attached to her the way she had to those babies.

Victoria had clear memories of being not more than three or four years old and having eleven-year-old Brooke brush her aside when she'd ask her for help or want to play with her. More often than not it had been teenage Eric who had silently helped her, but even he hadn't taken the time to play with her. And then he'd left.

Victoria pressed a hand to her chest as pain gripped her heart. Even now, she felt closer to Alicia than she did to Brooke. She dipped her head at the sting of tears. For whatever reason, her emotions were way too close to the surface tonight.

"You okay, Tori?"

The irony that it was Brooke who asked the question didn't escape Victoria. Pasting a smile on her face, she looked at her older sister and said, "Yep. So, what movie are we going to watch?"

There wasn't too much debate about the movie, and soon they'd all gotten tickets and the snacks they wanted.

As they walked toward the theater where the movie was being shown, Victoria began to wish she'd turned down the invitation. She just wasn't in the mood. Her emotions were in a bit of a mess, and not just because of her thoughts about Brooke. The whole computer situation had frustrated her, too. And then there was Trent.

Exposure to him in small doses—always with others around—had made it easy to brush aside his flirtations, but the one-on-one time had begun to change things for her. She had known that it would. That had been one of the main reasons she'd waited as long as she had to call him for help.

Unfortunately, it appeared that while spending time with Trent had Victoria reconsidering her feelings about them dating, it had had the opposite effect on him.

"So, that was a bit unexpected," Eric commented as he fell into step beside Trent. "Hearing you were at Tori's."

"Yeah. I was surprised when her number popped up on my phone earlier, but it was just because she needed help with her computer. Pretty sure she wouldn't have called me otherwise." He paused as they approached the theater. "I'll be there in a second. Save me a seat on the end."

Eric shot him a look but didn't argue as Staci pulled him toward the door. Trent hoped he would just think he needed to use the washroom or wanted more snacks. Trent didn't need either, but he did need to make sure that he was true to what he'd said to Victoria in order to get her to agree to come. No doubt because they'd arrived together, people would assume they wanted to sit next to each other. That would be way too much like a date for her. So he'd wait until they were all seated, and hopefully give Victoria time to maneuver things so there wasn't an empty seat next to her.

He moved in the direction of the washrooms just in case any of the group came back out. Feeling a little dumb, he walked into the bathroom, then turned around and walked back out. The things he did for Victoria. Truthfully, he would have been happy if they'd arranged it so he'd ended up seated next to her. However, he had a feeling that she would have been even more unhappy than usual with him if that had happened.

Walking slowly, he made his way back to the theater and stepped into the dimly lit interior. He paused for a moment to let his eyes adjust and then looked for the group. When he found them, he saw that his own maneuvering had worked. From what he could tell, Victoria was seated between Brooke and Alicia and there was an empty seat on the aisle beside Staci.

He sank down into the seat, setting his drink in the cup holder.

Staci smiled at him and leaned closer to ask, "Did you want to sit with Victoria?"

Trent shook his head. "I promised her this wouldn't be like a date, so it's better I don't."

"Ah. When Eric said you were over at her place I thought maybe..."

"No. Nothing like that. Believe me, I was the last person she wanted to call, but she needed my computer expertise." Trent stretched out his legs and relaxed back into the seat. "She did cook me supper, and I'm still alive so that's a positive thing."

Staci snickered. "I sincerely doubt she'd poison you."

"Well, at least not before her computer is fixed, but I told her I'd behave tonight so hopefully that will get me some brownie points." Trent sighed. "Would love to know her objection to dating me, but then again...maybe not."

Staci reached out and laid her hand on his arm. "You're a good man, Trent. If it's God's will, it will fall into place. I'll continue to pray for wisdom for both of you."

"Thanks." Trent covered her hand with his.

Eric leaned forward and said, "You flirting with my wife, Hause?"

"What? You mean because I'm holding her hand?" Trent laughed as Staci slid her hand from beneath his. "You know I'd never do that, dude. Plus, no one else in this whole wide world is even half the man you are. At least in her eyes."

Staci smiled as she lifted her hand and laid it on the side of her husband's face, stroking his cheek with her thumb. The absolute devotion in Eric's gaze as he turned his attention to her caused a tendril of jealousy to wind through Trent.

Thankfully, the theater's lights dimmed completely and the previews started. He laced his hands across his stomach and kept his gaze straight ahead. The movie wasn't bad, but it didn't quite capture his total attention. Too many times he found himself wondering if he should just come right out and ask Victoria what her objections were.

But he was afraid if he pushed too hard, she'd just shut him down altogether. Maybe if she realized that he was more than just jokes and lighthearted conversation, she might be willing to give him a shot. But in order for her to see that, they needed to spend time together. This computer situation was a good place to start.

Trent just really didn't want to hear that she wasn't interested in him because he was an average-size guy. There was nothing he could do about that. But he was more than his height, just like she was.

When the movie ended, Trent was the first to get up. He stretched and let some people go up the aisle before stepping out and heading toward the exit. Once out of the theater, he moved to the side to wait for others.

They gradually straggled out with the rest of the moviegoers. Trent didn't miss that like Eric and Staci, Lucas and Brooke were looking all lovey-dovey. He wondered how long it would be before there was another McKinley wedding. In fact, he was somewhat surprised that there hadn't already been an engagement announcement.

Alicia and Victoria were the last ones to come out of the theater. As the group moved toward the exit of the building, Trent was careful to hang around Eric.

"So how bad is the computer?" Eric asked as they stepped out into the warm evening air.

"I'm getting her a new one. That one she has is giving her error messages and making a horrible racket. It's definitely time for an upgrade."

Eric shot a look to where Victoria stood talking with Alicia. "Listen, whatever the cost is, tell her it's half. I'll cover the rest."

Trent raised his eyebrows. "I'll be building the system so it shouldn't be too expensive. I was only going to charge her for some of the parts anyway."

Eric grinned. "Well, between the two of us we should be able to keep it low cost for her. Just don't let her know. Get her what she needs."

"I will. No worries there. It would be a personal affront to my computer abilities to get her anything but the best."

"We're going to head off," Brooke announced. "Thanks for the invite, Eric."

Lucas kept his arm around Brooke as they said goodbye and then walked toward their car.

"You need a ride home, Tori?" Alicia asked as she pulled her keys from her pocket. "I might be convinced to make a detour to Dairy Queen."

"Tempting, but Trent left his laptop at my place so he's giving me a ride home. Plus, we already had dessert. That's got to be my limit for tonight."

Alicia looked from Victoria to Trent then to Eric and Staci and smiled. "Enjoy the rest of your evening."

"We plan to," Eric said with a grin. "And I think it will likely include a stop at the aforementioned Dairy Queen."

"See you guys," Staci called out as Eric took her by the hand and pulled her from the group.

Alicia bent to give Victoria a hug. Apparently, she said something while doing so because Victoria nodded and smiled when her sister straightened.

"I'll give you a call sometime this weekend," Alicia said with a wave as she headed toward the parking lot.

After doing his best to keep his distance all evening for her sake, Trent finally moved to Victoria's side. "You ready to head home?"

She nodded. "That was fun, but I'm tired."

Just as she stepped away from him, Trent's phone vibrated on his hip. He paused to check the screen and looked up in time to see a group of teenage boys walk by Victoria.

One of them bumped into her causing her to grab the metal railing on the stairs to keep from falling. Then, with a smirk clear on his face, the kid said, "Oh. Sorry. Didn't see you down there."

In two large strides, Trent was at Victoria's side. He glared at the group of young men. "That didn't sound quite as sincere as it should have."

"Trent." He felt a touch on his arm and looked down to see Victoria's hand there. She shook her head. "Don't."

CHAPTER FOUR

DON'T?" Anger swirled through Trent as his gaze went back the group of boys. "They're lucky all I'm doing is requesting a more sincere apology for their assault on you."

The boys laughed, and the one who'd bumped into Victoria scoffed. "Assault?"

"You intentionally bumped into her." Trent braced his legs and put his hands on his hips.

The offender took a step toward them and sneered at Trent. "Says who?"

When the teenager took another step in Victoria's direction, Trent reacted. Before the kid could even blink, Trent had covered the distance between them and had the kid's arm twisted up behind his back. They were the same height, but clearly Trent outweighed and outmuscled the kid.

"Says me," Trent growled in his ear. "You give the lady a more convincing apology and then you leave. You really, really don't want to mess with her—or me—any further."

The kid glanced at his friends who were now backing away, their eyes wide. Obviously recognizing that he was going to get no further support from that direction, his head dipped forward. "Sorry."

Trent gave him a shake. "I kinda doubt she heard that. How about you look her in the eye and say it again?"

The kid lifted his head slightly and looked in Tori's direction. "Sorry."

Trent's gaze met Victoria's, and she nodded.

He spun the kid around so he could look at him. "You need to spend some time thinking about what it is about you that makes picking on people who are smaller or weaker than you a pleasurable thing. Because in my book that makes you nothing more than a pathetic coward. Now get lost. All of you."

They didn't need a second invitation to leave the confrontation. Trent watched them go, his hands on his hips once again. When he was confident they wouldn't cause them any more problems, he relaxed his stance and looked to where Victoria stood. "Let's go."

He wished that he could hug her or somehow touch her to reassure her that she was safe. He would have done that with any other woman in the same situation, but something told him Victoria wouldn't appreciate the gesture. They walked in silence to his car where he retrieved her stool and waited as she climbed in to the front seat.

When he settled behind the steering wheel, he didn't start it right away. He could feel something—anger?—emanating off Victoria. And she was likely feeling the same thing from him.

"*Don't*, Victoria?" Trent gripped the wheel in both hands. "They were bullying you, and that's how you react? Why wouldn't you respond to that?"

He could hear the frustration in her sigh. "I usually just ignore it and move on. They're ignorant and not worth my time."

"You *usually*...?" Trent turned to look at her, wishing the sun hadn't started to go down so he could see her more clearly. "This has happened before?"

"Well, sure. It's a fact of life when you're different. It doesn't happen often, but it *does* happen."

"And you let them get away with it?" Trent asked, anger pumping through him with every beat of his heart.

"I'm not exactly in a position to take on a pack of teenage boys, now am I?" Irritation edged Victoria's words. "Ignoring them is the best way for me to deal with it. Letting them see that what they say or do upsets me only gives them satisfaction. I won't do that."

"Yeah, well, they're just lucky I didn't have my gun on me," Trent growled as he started the car up with a quick twist of his wrist.

"Your *gun*? You would have shot those kids?"

Trent let out an exasperated laugh. "No, but I might have used it to put the fear of God—or my gun—in them."

"From the look of it, you managed to scare them without having to point a weapon at them. And I'm saved from having to call Marcus Black to bail you out of jail for threatening them with a gun."

"Yeah, just these two guns," Trent said as he lifted first one arm and flexed it and then the other.

The anger slowly eased away when he heard Victoria chuckle. "But really, you own a gun?"

"Several, actually, but I only carry one with me." Trent backed out of the parking spot.

"Where is it?"

"In my laptop bag at your place."

"Seriously? Why do you carry a gun?"

Trent guided the Jeep out of the theater parking lot. "Marcus and Alex insist that all of us are trained in firearms and carry at least one weapon."

"At least one?"

"Most of us just carry a gun, but some—namely Justin—carry two guns or—depending on the situation—a gun and a knife."

"Wow. I guess I must have misunderstood what you guys at BlackThorpe do. Eric has a gun, too?"

"Sure. He also has more than one. All of which I know he keeps well out of Sarah's reach."

"Is the work you do that dangerous?"

Trent glanced at her. "My particular line of work doesn't put me on the front line like some of the other guys, but our clients and the information we have makes all of us a potential target. Marcus expects each of us to be able to take care of ourselves should something happen."

"I guess I never realized..." She paused and then said, "I've always wanted to learn to shoot a gun."

Trent chuckled. "Well, if you're serious, I can make that happen for you."

"Yeah, I'm serious, but I still won't take on punks like those guys tonight."

"Good idea. I'd rather not have to bail *you* out of jail because you shot some idiot who ran his mouth off at you."

"I still can't believe you and Eric have guns," Victoria said. "And thank you, by the way. I do appreciate you standing up for me."

"Anytime, babe. Anytime."

As Trent pulled into her driveway, Victoria had to admit she was a bit disappointed that the evening was over. Though it had had its ups and downs, she'd seen different sides to Trent that she hadn't been aware of before. Yeah, the fun, flirty side had still been present, but she'd also seen him be more serious and caring. And then the protective side had come out full force during that confrontation with the teenage boys.

"If you pop your trunk, I'll put the stool back and then come in to get my bag."

Victoria pulled out her keys while she waited for him to get her stool. She hit the button to open the trunk and then slid from the seat to the stool. Once she was on the ground, he easily picked it up and moved toward her car. She went on into the house, leaving the door open behind her.

"I will be working on your computer tomorrow," Trent said as he came in and shut the door. "When would be a good time to bring it by?"

"You don't need to spend your Saturday working on that," Victoria protested. "I do have a laptop that I can use until you're done. So there's no rush."

Trent shrugged. "I didn't really have anything important planned tomorrow. I had thought about going out to the compound to spar with Justin, but I can do that anytime."

"The compound? Spar?" Victoria asked.

"BlackThorpe has a rural property where they train people. That's where the gun range is, among other things. Justin helps me with my physical training. Technically it's called sparring, but I usually just call it *Justin beating me up*. Which is why I'm more than happy to do computer work instead. He's not gonna argue with me if I tell him I need to help Eric's sister out."

"Well, if it will save you from a beating then I won't protest you spending your Saturday on my computer. And anytime is usually fine. I'm at church Sunday morning and have a couple of appointments next week, but I should be home most evenings."

Trent bent over to pick up his bag from where he'd left it earlier. "I'll give you a call once it's ready to go."

"Thank you. I really do appreciate you helping me with this. Especially since I haven't always been...friendly."

Trent smiled at her, creases bracketing his mouth. "I'm sure you have your reasons. But no worries, I have no expectations because I'm helping you. Dinner was payment enough."

"Not hardly," Victoria said with a laugh.

"Hey, don't discount the pleasure a home-cooked meal brings a single man. Why do you think I accept every invitation Eric issues to a family event? Your mom is a great cook, and it appears she's passed that on to you."

"Well, then if you give me enough of a heads up, I could probably make a meal for you when you come drop it off."

"Sounds like a plan." Trent turned toward the door. "I'd better go. I'll give you a call about the computer."

Victoria followed him to the door and then out onto the porch. "Thank you again. For everything."

This was one of those times when she hated her lack of height. If she'd been an average-size woman, she could have given him a quick, friendly hug, but hugs were a bit awkward unless he bent down to her level. She wasn't about to ask him to do that and something told her he wouldn't be initiating that contact either.

"You're welcome. Stay safe."

As he walked down the porch steps, Victoria went back inside and shut the door. She flipped the locks then leaned back against it. As she stood there, she took a deep breath and willed herself to relax.

Pushing away from the door so she could lock it, she allowed herself to grimace at the pain that was throbbing in her hip. She opened the closet near the door and pulled her crutches from behind the coats. After getting them on properly, she moved with considerably less pain toward her bedroom.

Victoria hadn't given much thought to how long it might take Trent to get back to her, but she hadn't expected him to call her Sunday afternoon to let her know it was ready.

"Wow. That was quick."

"Well, like I said, I didn't have anything else to do that couldn't be put off, and I managed to get all the parts I needed. When do you want me to come drop it off?"

"I'm home the rest of today and any evening this week. Whatever works for you."

"Okay. I'll be by in about an hour. Shouldn't take too long to get it set up and running."

As she hung up, Victoria wondered if he'd worked on it so quickly in order to get it over with. He hadn't even given her enough time to make a meal for him like she'd promised. And she was sweaty and gross from working out in the yard after she'd gotten home from lunch at her mom and dad's.

There was no contest between taking a shower or throwing a meal together. The shower won out, hands down.

She might not be dressing to impress him, but she also wasn't going to look like a slob.

Trent stepped from his car, inhaling the scent of freshly mowed grass that hung in the warm summer air. He opened the door to retrieve the tower and the peripherals he'd bought for it from the back seat. She wasn't going to be too pleased with them most likely, but her monitor was way too small, and he'd noticed that some of the letters were beginning to wear off on her keyboard. If she was going to upgrade, might as well do it across the board, particularly since she wouldn't be shouldering one hundred percent of the cost.

Shifting the tower to free up his hand, Trent pressed the doorbell and waited. As he stood there, he heard a lawnmower fire up in the distance. It was far enough away that it didn't drown out the sounds of children at play and dogs barking. These were all the sounds of neighborhood living that he missed out on in his apartment.

The door swung open, drawing his attention. "Hey, Victoria."

"Hi, Trent. Come on in." She stepped back.

As he walked past her, Trent noticed that a light floral scent hung in the air. She wore a white blouse that was tied at her waist and open over top of a dress that reached her ankles. Her hair hung in straight silky strands across her shoulders and appeared to be slightly damp like she'd just gotten out of the shower.

Pushing aside his thoughts on her appearance, Trent walked to her desk and set down the tower and other things he'd brought.

"That's more than just a computer," Victoria commented when she joined him.

"Everything needed an upgrade." He gestured to the keyboard. "You do realize that you've worn off some of the letters on that thing, right?"

"Sure, but I don't look at the keys when I type so it wasn't a big deal."

Trent laughed. "Still. I think it was time for a new one. And your monitor is pretty much obsolete."

"From what you're saying, the whole system is obsolete." Victoria rested her arm on the desk which was at just the right height for her.

As he sat down on the office chair, Trent grinned at her. "Babe, that system was obsolete within about a year after you bought it. Computers have rapidly evolved over the past few years."

"I don't necessarily need to have the fastest computer with the biggest hard drive, do I?"

"No, you probably don't need that, and that's not what I've given you here. If you ever get into gaming or doing a lot of graphic intensive stuff, we can revisit your computing needs."

"That's not going to happen."

"You never know."

"Are you into gaming?" she asked as he bent to unhook the cords from the old tower.

"I used to be. I've kind of outgrown it now, though I do step back into it from time to time if I'm really bored. I'd actually rather do this kind of stuff." He gestured to the new tower.

"You didn't give me time to prepare a meal as a way to say thanks."

"Some other time." Trent smiled at her before turning his attention back to the old tower. When she didn't respond, he glanced back to find her watching him, her expression serious. "What?"

"I just feel like I'm taking advantage of you. It doesn't feel right."

Trent pulled the tower out and set it aside then lifted the old monitor off the desk. "Can't take advantage of me when I'm offering my services so don't worry about it."

"Still."

He sat back in the chair and looked at her. Lifting his hands, he said, "No strings. I promise. I'm happy to have this to do. It's not like you asked me to shovel out a horse stall or something like that. I probably would have still done it but wouldn't have enjoyed it nearly as much."

Trent wished he could read what was going on in that head of hers, but her expression gave nothing away. He reached for the box that held the new monitor. "Do you have a pair of scissors?"

"In the drawer there." Victoria pointed to the side of the desk.

Trent pulled it open and leaned over to look into the drawer. He spotted the scissors almost immediately but then spotted something else. "Hey, I never did see the pictures from Eric's wedding."

"Uh, yeah, my mom gave me some copies of the pictures the photographer took."

Trent took the photo from the drawer, his mind going back to that day. This particular pose had obviously been taken while he and Victoria had been negotiating their positions for the picture. They were looking at each other and smiling. He remembered how his heartbeat had kicked up a notch when she'd smiled at him before the photographer had called for their attention. He hadn't realized the guy had taken that shot before the more formal pose.

Though the image on the photo was now burned in his memory, he was going to have to see if he could get a copy of it for himself. Slowly, he put the picture back, retrieved the scissors and closed the drawer. He didn't look at her as he tackled the tape that held the monitor box closed. No doubt she was waiting for him to make some flippant comment about the picture, but he wasn't going to take that route this time.

CHAPTER FIVE

HERE, can you open these things for me?" Trent bent and picked up the packages containing the keyboard and mouse.

"Sure." She took the items from him and moved over to the coffee table where there was more room for her to work.

Over the course of the last day, Trent had decided that a different approach was needed when it came to Victoria. For the past several months, he'd tried to get her attention by flirting with her and being around where she was. He'd felt a bit like a teenager with a crush. All that had done was make her skittish and wary of him. So much so that she'd risked all the information on her computer before finally biting the bullet and calling him.

Clearly, he needed to just back off and let her become more comfortable with him and then see where things went. He had nothing to lose by changing tactics. It wasn't like the way he'd approached things so far had been working for him. In fact, it had probably worked against him. Not that he could completely turn off the teasing banter, that was just part of who he was, but he needed her to see him in a more serious light if he was going to have any chance at all.

They'd been working in silence for a few minutes when he suddenly heard music playing softly. He looked over to see that Victoria had hooked her phone up to some speakers. The song was familiar to him as they'd just sung it that morning in church. Humming along, he sat down on the floor and ducked under the desk to get the monitor and tower plugged in.

"Here you go."

He made sure he was clear of the desk before straightening. As he did, he found himself in the rather odd and unusual position of looking up to Victoria. She held out the keyboard and mouse, now free of their packaging.

Their positioning must have struck her as well because she grinned. "I think this is the first time I've seen the top of your head."

Trent ran a hand through his hair and returned her grin. "Thankfully, I'm putting my best hair forward today. Would've been a shame if the first time you saw the top of my head my hair was a mess or I was bald."

She tilted her head. "Well, you're definitely not bald."

Before he could respond, he heard the doorbell ring. Victoria's brows drew together as she turned away from him. "I'll be right back."

As he plugged the keyboard in, he heard a child's voice greet Victoria.

"Hey, Tori!"

"Hi, Bridgie. How are you?"

"I'm good. Mom sent me to see if you want to come over. Dad's barbecuing, and Uncle Seth is there, too."

"Thanks for the invite, sweetie, but please tell your mom I can't come over tonight."

"You can't? Why not?" Disappointment was clear in the girl's voice.

"I have company at the moment."

"That their car in your driveway?"

"Yes, that's his car. So just tell your mom maybe another time, okay?"

"Is he your boyfriend?"

"Who?"

"The dude whose car is in your driveway."

"No. He's a friend who's helping me with some stuff today."

"Okay. That's good. Mom really wants you to hook up with Uncle Seth."

Trent glanced over at that comment, but there was a wall between him and the door so he couldn't get a glimpse of the kid.

"Well, tell your mom to call me this week and we'll chat about that."

"Cool! See ya!"

Trent heard the door shut and quickly returned his attention to the computer. When Victoria came back to the desk, he said, "You know, if you want to go to your neighbor's, I'm almost done here. I can come back another day to show you all the ins and outs."

Victoria's eyebrows rose and then lowered again as they drew together. "No, I'm perfectly fine having an excuse not to accept that particular invitation."

"Not interested in hooking up with Uncle Seth?" he said as he ducked under the desk but not before seeing the scowl on Victoria's face.

"Fran seems to think that just because her brother is a little person that I should be happy to date him."

"He's a little person, too?"

"Yeah." Victoria sighed. "She's been after me to meet her brother since she moved into the neighborhood six months ago. I've managed to avoid it so far."

Trent glanced over at her. "Why don't you want to meet him?"

"Because of other things she'd said about him. And hooking up? I'm not interested in hooking up with any guy. I don't just automatically date every male little person that comes along. In fact, that's not even on my list of things I want in a guy."

"So you don't judge a guy's date-ability based on his height or lack thereof?" Trent stuck his head back under the desk.

"Of course not." He smiled at the indignant tone in her voice. "I'm much more likely to judge a guy's date-ability based on the size of his bank account."

Trent jerked his head up, wincing as it connected with the desk above him. Rubbing the spot, he sat back and shot Victoria a look. "Say what?"

Crossing her arms, she smiled at him.

"Brat," Trent said with a frown in her direction before returning his attention to the tower.

"Hey, you asked for that one."

Trent supposed that he had, but at least he'd come away from the exchange knowing that she wasn't holding his height against him. So it must be something else.

"Did you want something to drink?"

"Sure. Whatever's cold."

He heard her move away but didn't look at her again. Her teasing was sorely trying his resolution to be more serious in his interactions with her. By the time she came back with a drink for him, he had the keyboard and mouse hooked up and had turned on the machine. He settled onto the chair again as the tower beeped and the monitor came to life.

"That's a lot bigger than my old one," Victoria said as she placed a bottle of his favorite soda next to the keyboard.

It shouldn't have pleased him so much that she knew what he liked—after all, it was pretty much the only thing he drank—and had it on hand, but it still warmed him. "Yes, it is. As I said, your whole setup was out of date. I'll be making sure that doesn't happen again."

He clicked a few different icons to check the settings and then slid from the chair. "Here. Why don't you have a seat so I can show you what I've got set up."

When Victoria was settled into the chair, he lowered himself to one knee, bracing his arm along the back of her seat. He pointed to an icon on the monitor. "Let's start there."

After about five minutes of showing her the different programs he'd installed, Victoria said, "I sure hope I can remember all this. I feel like I should be taking notes."

"You don't really need to remember in detail." Trent glanced at her just as she turned her head. Given their positions, they were pretty much at eye level with each other.

Their gazes met and held. They were close enough he could see the dark ring around the outside of her irises and the flecks of black in her brown eyes. When her gaze dropped to his mouth momentarily, Trent felt his heart thud in his chest. But no matter how much his body clamored to make that physical connection to Victoria through a kiss, he knew it wasn't the time. And he didn't have that right. Not yet.

Clearing his throat, Trent looked back at the screen and tried to remember what he had been about to say. "Uh...actually, most of these programs I've set up run on their own at certain times. Your system will automatically back up your whole hard drive each night, and I've set it up to do virus scans on a regular basis. You don't have to do anything, but I wanted you to be aware of what was going on with your system."

"And all my other programs are still here?" Victoria's voice was softer than usual.

"Yes, I reloaded all the programs from your old system and then used the backup I did yesterday to make sure all your files were intact." Trent tried to keep focused on the matter at hand, but Victoria's nearness, the soft scent of whatever shampoo or soap or perfume she wore, and how he felt about her were making that a huge challenge. Maybe another guy would have taken advantage of the opportunity to kiss her, but Trent didn't want to do that.

Well, technically he *did*—he was a guy, after all—but he also knew it would complicate a situation that had been anything but simple right from the start. If they kissed—no, *when* they kissed—it would be a choice they made with the security of a relationship between them. Until then, he needed to make sure he resisted the temptation to give in to something that had no place in how things currently were between them.

"Do you have any other questions about the setup?" He looked at her, but this time Victoria was keeping her gaze on the screen.

"Is my printer ready to go, too? I need to be able to print invoices and such."

"Ah, forgot about that." Trent got to his feet. "I can do that right now."

Victoria slid off the chair and moved a couple of steps away. "Is it difficult to set up a new printer if I were to get one?"

"No, not at all." Trent wanted to kick himself for not thinking about adding a printer to the setup he'd done for her. "If you decide to get one, just give me a call. I can either walk you through it or stop by and set it up for you."

"I should probably learn how to do this stuff for myself," Victoria said, her gaze still on the computer screen.

"There's no need for that when I'm just a phone call away," Trent said as he clicked on the icon to bring up the printer screen. For some reason, it was important to him that there be something in her life that she relied on him for. Where some people may have used something like dwarfism as an excuse for not doing things, Victoria had made it clear that it wasn't something that would stop her. He admired that, but still he wanted to be able to do something for her.

Her cell phone rang as he worked, and the music that had been playing ended abruptly when she answered it. "Hi, Eric."

Trent winced as he heard her greet his friend. When they'd talked at church that morning, he hadn't mentioned that he was coming over to Victoria's again. He wasn't sure why he hadn't told him about it, but he figured Victoria was going to.

"Just learning about my new computer. Trent's here getting it all set up."

It was more than a little frustrating to only get half the conversation, Trent mused as he prepared to print a test page.

"Tomorrow? Yeah, that should be fine. It's my grocery shopping day with Mom, but we can just bring Sarah along." She paused. "Yep, I'm sure. If nothing else, I'll bribe her with making cookies when we get home if she's good."

She'll be a great mom.

The thought popped into Trent's head out of the blue, and he blinked a couple of times trying to figure out where it had come from. He'd seen her maternal side before in relation to Sarah and Danny. It was just one of the many things that had drawn him to her. Even before they'd met, Trent had determined that whatever woman he eventually married would have to show herself to be good mom material. There was no way he was going to let any child of his endure the negligence he'd experienced as a kid.

"Okay, I'll tell him. See you tomorrow."

"Babysitting duty?" Trent asked he looked at the test page the printer had just spat out.

"Yep. Seems Staci has a couple of appointments she can't take Sarah to."

Trent swung the chair around to look at Victoria, confident her system was now completely set up. "You enjoy babysitting her?"

"Sure. She's a firecracker though." Victoria smiled. "Keeps me on my toes. I never imagined that there would be someone in our family like me without them being my own child. Although people often do assume she's mine when I'm out with her."

"Do you hope to have children someday?" Trent asked.

Her gaze flitted away from his for a moment and when she looked back at him, he couldn't read anything on her face. She shrugged. "I go back and forth on that. When I had to have surgeries when I was younger, I swore I'd never chance having a child knowing that they might have to go through what I did. But when I'm not in the midst of the pain of the surgeries and when I see Sarah... Well, I think it might be nice to have one or two."

"Is it a guarantee that any child you have will inherit dwarfism? I mean, neither of your parents or Eric or Staci were little people, and yet you and Sarah both are. Does it work the other way, too?"

"There is definitely a higher probability that any child I have or Sarah has will have dwarfism. And that probability rises if the father is also a little person. But two little people can also have an average-size child."

"Well, I'm sure you'll make a great mom either way." Trent picked up his soda and took a long drink trying to ease the dryness in his mouth.

"Only time will tell." Her gaze went past him to the computer. "So, is the printer all set up?"

Trent swung the chair back around and picked up the test paper. "Yep. I should have thought to pick up a new printer for you, too. I'm surprised you can still get ink for this one."

"I will likely buy one soon." She walked over to the desk. "So how much is the total for all this?"

Trent hesitated. He really wanted to tell her it was taken care of, but he had a feeling she'd balk at that. "I have the receipts at home. I'll email you a total later tonight."

"Thank you. And tack on some for your time."

He looked at her and gave her a half grin. "You couldn't afford my time, babe."

Her eyes widened briefly at his statement. "Guess BlackThorpe pays you well?"

"You better believe it." Trent bent to gather up the old parts and put them in the monitor box to be disposed of later. "But I would likely do the job for free because I enjoy it so much."

"That wouldn't pay the bills."

He gave her a quick grin as he stood up. "Yeah, but my trust fund would."

This time, in addition to her eyes widening, her jaw dropped a little. Trent reached out and tapped her under her chin and winked. "Let's just say that if you really were judging a man by the size of his bank account, I'd be your guy."

"You do realize I was just joking, right? I didn't know..."

Trent laughed. "Of course, I know you were joking. No one but Marcus and Alex know the true state of my finances, and they only know because of that background check they do on all of us. Well, you know now, too."

"I won't tell anyone. I promise." The serious look on her face made him chuckle again.

"It wouldn't really matter if you did. I just prefer people not know because they start to treat you differently when they realize you have money." He lifted an eyebrow at her. "Although maybe having you treat me differently might not be a bad thing."

She stared at him for a moment before a grin spread across her face. "Well, that's not gonna happen just because you have money."

Her response didn't surprise him, but he was kind of glad for it. For some women, finding out about his money would have made him suddenly more interesting. In actuality, he didn't touch his trust fund money. He hadn't lied when he said BlackThorpe paid him well. He had more than enough for the fairly simple lifestyle that he chose to lead. All he really needed was the best computer money could buy and a comfortable bed, and he was set.

"I'm just gonna take this stuff out to the car. I'll dispose of it later."

As he stepped out onto the porch, the scent of barbecue tantalized his senses. Likely the smells were coming from the house where Victoria had been invited to go. He loaded the old computer into the back of his Jeep and then returned to the house.

As he closed the door behind him, Trent spotted Victoria walking toward the kitchen and noticed again a bit of a hitch in her step. Maybe it hadn't been his imagination last time. He knew some people with dwarfism had difficulty walking, but that had never seemed to be the case with Victoria in the years he'd known her. It concerned him, but he didn't want to say anything in case it really was nothing.

"I guess that's it," he said as he picked up the last of the trash from the packaging they'd opened earlier. "If you have any problems or questions about anything, feel free to give me a call."

"Thank you again for helping me." The smile she gave him kicked his heartbeat up a notch.

"Next time don't wait so long," he chided her. "You could have lost a lot of your data."

She lifted a hand to tuck a strand of her hair behind her ear. "Yeah. I've learned my lesson."

"Good. And it wasn't so bad having me around for a bit, was it? I know when to behave myself."

She laughed. "Yes. I was pleasantly surprised. Which is good, because I still owe you a dinner."

"And I do plan to collect," Trent assured her. "But since you just fed me a delicious meal the other night, I'm going to spread the goodness out a bit."

"Just let me know when you want it."

As they walked to the front door, Trent watched her out of the corner of his eye. Though the limp didn't reappear, he noticed that her mouth had tightened into a firm line.

"Wow, I can smell the barbecue," she said as they stepped out onto the porch.

"I'm sure the invitation to join them still stands." Trent pressed the button on his fob to unlock the Jeep.

"Oh no." Victoria shook her head vigorously. "I'm going to lock my door and not answer it again tonight. Uncle Seth can find someone else to hook up with."

Trent thought about suggesting he stick around, but he didn't want to press her when things seemed to be going so well. "Have a good evening."

"You, too."

With a last smile at her, Trent headed down the porch steps to his car. He wasn't thrilled about returning to his quiet apartment so he turned in the direction of the compound instead. No doubt Justin would be hanging around since the guy seemed to live out there. A good sparring session seemed the perfect way to burn off some of the frustration he felt when it came to his relationship—or lack thereof—with Victoria.

CHAPTER SIX

AFTER locking the door, Victoria walked back into her living room. She rubbed at her left hip, hating that it was becoming more and more clear that she was going to have surgery again. With a sigh, she settled on the couch with her legs stretched out across it, a pillow behind her back.

She was still trying to absorb all that she'd learned about Trent over the course of the past couple of hours. Never in a million years would she have pegged him as a trust fund guy even though he'd mentioned that his family had money. Oh, she'd known he wasn't poor. Just by being around Eric, she knew that BlackThorpe paid its employees well, so she hadn't really thought much about Trent's financial status.

Victoria wondered what it would be like to not have to worry about money. Unfortunately, it was a major issue for her, particularly when it came to her surgery. The deductible for the insurance she had was high, and even though she'd been putting aside money in case surgery became necessary, she knew what she had wasn't nearly enough. And she wouldn't share that information with her family or she'd end up being a charity case, and they'd already done so much for her.

She was grateful that the house she lived in cost her nothing. Her dad had inherited it after the death of his mother, but they'd already had a home they loved. They'd offered it to Brooke, but she'd outright refused it since she wasn't interested in taking anything from their dad at that time. They'd rented it out for a while and then when Victoria had wanted to move out on her own, they'd given it to her to live in. It had been a blessing in that she could have her independence without spending a lot on rent.

Victoria lifted her arm to cover her eyes. Some days she really wished that all she had to worry about was planning for a future with a husband and children. Unfortunately, she had so much more than that to have to consider. Being with Trent, having him help her the way he had, had brought to life a longing to have someone at her side.

For as long as she could remember, Victoria had tried so hard to prove that she could do it all, that her dwarfism didn't hinder her from being able to do everything. But she was tired of that. Frankly, there *were* things that were just more difficult for her to do. Things she didn't like to do, and things that would be easier to tackle if she had someone by her side. Someone who loved her and didn't mind that sometimes she just *couldn't* do it all.

But the flip side was that things like this impending surgery made her a burden. Though Trent had seemed interested in taking things to another level with her, he'd had no clue what that would have involved now that surgery loomed in the not too distant future. But surgery or not, something had changed for him.

The time spent with him over the past two days hadn't helped her to have clarity on the issue at all. At times, he'd appeared to be flirting with her but then when things seemed to get a little more intense, he'd backed right off. Like when he'd found that picture of the two of them. She'd expected more of a reaction, a teasing comment about how good they looked together or something, but instead he'd just slid it back into the drawer.

He'd left her confused. Not that she hadn't already been confused by her own feelings where he was concerned, but now she was confused about *his* feelings for her.

She had to just focus on one thing at a time. First, she had a proposal she needed to put together. If it was accepted, the money from that would go a long ways to helping with the finances needed for her surgery. Once that was done, then maybe she could look toward a future that included a relationship with someone. Whether that someone would be Trent or not, she had no idea.

By Friday afternoon, Victoria was finishing off the last of a proposal. It was a presentation for a hotel chain about putting some of the products her company had developed in their hotels across the US and Canada. She'd put together a packet of information on which products she thought would be most useful in their hotels for little people or people with limited mobility who might be staying there. If they ordered three or four kits for each of their hotels, it would help her immensely. Up to this point, she'd only had success in getting individual places to buy a kit or two. Having a chain interested in purchasing for all their hotels would be such a boost to the company.

If they decided not to go through with it... Well, she didn't really want to think of that possibility.

Her cell phone rang as she clicked to save the document. Victoria stared for a moment when she saw it was Trent's number on the display, then slowly tapped the screen and pressed the phone to her ear.

"So how's the computer working?" Trent asked.

"Very well, thank you. Just finished working on something, and it was nice to not have to worry that an error message was going to pop up on me."

"No issues with the backup or virus scanning? I set them to start around three in the morning so they wouldn't interfere with any work you might need to do. Of course, I probably should have made sure you didn't do a lot of work at that time of night."

"Oh, that's fine. I'm not up that late ever."

"Neither am I," Trent said. "At least not by my choice."

"You still need to send me the bill for this machine," Victoria reminded him.

There was silence and then he said, "Yeah, I keep forgetting about that. I'll try and get to it this weekend."

"Well, I don't want to keep bugging you, but I also don't like to not pay when I owe someone."

There was another beat of silence and then he said, "How about we do a trade?"

"A trade?" Victoria leaned back in her chair. "What sort of trade?"

"How about we agree to some home-cooked meals and some baking. Kind of like what you sent with Eric on Tuesday. Thank you for the cookies, by the way. They were delicious."

Victoria felt a rush of pleasure at his words. "You're welcome. They were the cookies I made with Sarah while I babysat her on Monday. I'm glad you liked them."

"Which is why I'm suggesting a trade. A few home-cooked meals and some baking for the computer."

"That would take forever for me to work off." Plus, Victoria didn't know if she could handle spending that much time with Trent.

"Not really. As I said before, you apparently don't realize the value of a home-cooked meal, especially to a guy who eats way more takeout and fast food than he should. You're rather jaded in that regard because of having grown up with someone like your mom who cooked good food for you. My meals growing up were more likely to consist of some fancy French dish. You know the ones where everything is so small that nothing touches anything else on the plate?"

"Yeah, I've always wondered how people survived eating like that."

"Well, I didn't. I used to take my money and buy a loaf of bread and a jar of cheese spread to eat after those meals because they were unfulfilling on so many levels. So for me, the value of a home-cooked meal is fairly high."

"What exactly were you thinking then?"

"How about some cookies and a meal once a week for a month?"

Once a week for a month? She still thought she was getting off easy, but this was his deal. "And will you tell me what you want to eat?"

"Nope, that's entirely up to you."

When she thought of how she could funnel the money from the computer into her savings account, it suddenly became more appealing. Sure she'd have to spend a little extra on groceries, but not a lot. And she could compensate in other areas. So from a financial standpoint, it was definitely worth considering. It was just the emotional cost that worried her a bit.

But in the end, the thought of adding money to her savings account for the surgery won out. "Okay. That's a deal."

"Nice!" The pleasure in his voice warmed her. "So, are you free tomorrow?"

Her traitorous heart skipped a beat at the prospect of seeing him again. "You want to have dinner tomorrow night?"

"Yes, but I was also going to see if you were interested in going to the compound with me to do some shooting."

"Shooting?"

"You mentioned the other night that you'd always wanted to learn to shoot. I was thinking maybe we could go out to the company compound for a couple of hours, and you could see how you like it. Then go back to your place for dinner afterward."

She felt far more excited about his suggestion than she should have. "That sounds like fun."

"Good. How about I pick you up around two thirty? And I can help you with supper when we get back if you want."

"Nope. The deal is I cook and that's what I'll do. I have some ideas on how to make it work even if we go out to the compound. Just tell me now if there's anything you really don't like or are allergic to."

"No allergies that I'm aware of. There's nothing that I really hate to eat, but I will admit to not having a real fondness for brussels sprouts or asparagus."

"I will keep that in mind."

Trent chuckled. "I'll see you tomorrow."

As Victoria hung up, she wondered if she'd just bitten off way more than she could chew.

Victoria was up early Saturday morning to start the meal she decided to serve Trent after their time at the shooting range. It didn't take long to brown up the ground beef for the spaghetti sauce she planned to leave simmering in her slow cooker until they got back. She also started a batch of French bread and mixed up the crisp part of the apple crisp she would make later.

Once that was all underway, she took a quick shower and applied a light amount of makeup. This wasn't a date, after all, but that didn't stop her from spending far too long trying to figure out what to wear. What *did* a girl wear to a gun range? She'd spent some time the night before watching some videos on the internet about guns and shooting.

One had mentioned something about hot brass—which she'd learned was the spent shell casings—and how it didn't work well with a low-cut shirt. Not that she wore low-cut things, but the warning made her look more critically at the possible choices she had.

In the end, she settled on a pair of dark blue jean capris, a hot pink tank top and a pink plaid button-up shirt that she belted and left the top few buttons undone. She was glad that her mom had a knack for sewing. Most of her clothes needed some kind of alteration, and her mom was able to do whatever was necessary so Victoria didn't look like a kid playing dress-up. Or worse, having to wear clothing styles more suited to an eight-year-old.

By two o'clock, the rich, tangy tomato scent of the spaghetti sauce mingled with the freshly baked French bread causing her stomach to rumble appreciatively. She just hoped that Trent would agree. All she'd have to do upon their return would be to make the salad and the noodles.

After giving the sauce a final stir and making sure the slow cooker was set on low, Victoria went in search of appropriate footwear. Though she usually wore shoes that had some sort of heel, everything she'd read had said to wear practical shoes. So she'd settled for a pair of flat low-top, black lace-up shoes. The last thing she wanted to do was show up at the gun range dressed inappropriately, so she'd sacrifice fashion for practicality.

When she answered the door at precisely two thirty, Trent's gaze traveled the length of her body, clearly taking in what she wore. She felt her cheeks flush under his gaze.

He smiled as he said, "Perfect. I was afraid I might have to ask you to change."

"Good. I wasn't sure what exactly one wore to a gun range."

"What you've got on is just fine." He sniffed the air. "And whatever you're cooking smells fine, too."

Grinning, Victoria looped her purse over her shoulder and pulled the door shut behind her as she stepped out onto the porch. "You're gonna have to wait for that."

"Definitely something to look forward to," Trent said as they walked toward his car.

She popped the trunk of her car so he could get the stool out again. The August afternoon air was warm so the coolness of his car felt good as she climbed in and buckled the seatbelt.

"How far away is the place we're going?" Victoria asked as he braced his hand on her seat to back out of her driveway.

"About thirty minutes depending on traffic."

Victoria watched as he deftly maneuvered the wheel and soon they were on the main highway heading west. "How was your week?"

Trent glanced at her, but she couldn't see his eyes because of the sunglasses he wore. "It was good. A few glitches to take care of but nothing I couldn't handle."

The grin that curved his lips set her heart racing. She wasn't happy that he was having this effect on her and tried to keep her thoughts from completely scrambling because of it. "What exactly do you do at BlackThorpe?"

"I oversee a group of five computer geniuses. Three of them specialize in creating security programs and protocols for businesses. The other two work more with sensitive security issues. We monitor the security systems for businesses and also do other computer work as required."

"Hacking?"

Trent sent her another one of his grins. "We don't like to use that term. It's more like information reconnaissance and gathering."

"Aren't you afraid of getting caught?"

Trent shook his head. "We're not hacking into government systems. For the most part, the systems we gain access to involve illegal activities to begin with so it's not likely they're going to call the cyber police on us. And we are very good at what we do."

"I can't quite figure out if BlackThorpe is scary or benign. I mean, you guys walk around in suits and ties with briefcases. But then I find out you're all armed which makes me think you believe that danger lurks around every corner."

"Truthfully, different parts of the company involve more danger than others. I spend most my time in the office, so my job doesn't hold the physical risk of the others. Where we're going now is Justin's territory. We have teams come in for training on a regular basis."

"Teams?" Victoria found herself a lot more interested in BlackThorpe now that she was spending time with Trent even though Eric had worked there for several years.

"Special ops teams come to train for overseas missions. We have security teams come in for training when traveling with business personnel around the world. Justin has a group of six men who help with the training and then he has two other teams of six who actually go out on security missions."

"Do you spend a lot of time where we're going?"

"I go about once a week. We have a gym at the office so I make use of that, but Marcus likes us to keep up on our combat proficiency. Justin makes sure we stay in shape." Trent lifted his hand from the wheel and smiled as he flexed his arm. "Even us computer nerds."

Victoria smiled and then turned to look out the window at her side. Though Trent had always been an attractive man, his appeal to her was growing as she spent more time with him. That was going to be a dangerous thing. Though she had told him height wasn't an issue when it came to a guy, that wasn't entirely the truth.

All things being equal, she really didn't have a preference when it came to dating an average person versus a little person. But, unfortunately, all things weren't equal. She was used to being stared at and whispered about, but none of that really got any worse when she dated a guy who was also a little person. Her experience in dating average-size guys had been completely different when it came to the public's reaction.

The first guy had been at the start of her senior year in high school. They hadn't been going out for very long before rumors started to float around school about the guy. Things like he must like little girls since he was dating her. It was more than the guy could handle, and he'd dropped her like a hot potato.

Two years ago, she'd decided to give it another try when a man at church had asked her out. She had assumed it had just been because of the immaturity of the first guy that he hadn't been able to handle a few whispered rumors. But when the same thing had happened again, Victoria realized that it just might be more than any man could really handle.

No guy in his right mind would want to be known as liking little girls just because he chose to date her.

Though it was tempting, Victoria just wasn't sure if she was ready to try again for the third time. Particularly since Trent was her brother's friend. If things went south like they had with the other average-size guys she'd dated, it would be way more awkward. So, in spite of all that her heart was telling her, Victoria knew she needed to keep things on a friendship level.

Thankfully, Trent seemed to have pulled back from his overt flirting. That would make it a bit easier.

"This is also BlackThorpe land," Trent said as he turned down a rural road. "That building there is where Melanie Thorpe works with the wounded warriors."

"Wounded warriors?"

"Yes, since both Alex and Marcus are ex-military, they set it up to help other veterans. They offer support for the physical, emotion and mental struggles that a vet might have. Lots of the guys who come through there are struggling with things like PTSD. They have psychologists on hand to help them. They also have physical therapists to help with the physically wounded vets. Some need prosthetics or help learning to do things again after a severe injury."

"That's great that they give back that way."

"Yes, it is, and Melanie is amazing in the work she does. She and Adrianne do a lot of fundraising for the organization in order to help more vets. Mel's a quiet one, but when she believes in something, she goes after it full force."

Victoria couldn't believe the twinge of jealousy she felt when she heard the admiration in Trent's voice. This really, really wasn't good.

"I try to volunteer there once a month or so," Trent continued.

"What do you do?"

"Depends who's in residence when I go. Sometimes we play ball or maybe some video games. Sometimes it's just talking to them. If nothing else, I walk a dog."

"They have a dog there?"

"More than one actually. Last time I was there they had four. A couple were retired military dogs. The other two were trained service dogs. It seems that sometimes the dogs can calm and ground a guy more than anything else."

"I've heard that before," Victoria said. "And I've seen them using dogs in hospitals."

"Here we are." Trent slowed the vehicle and turned into a driveway that was blocked by a large gate.

As Victoria looked more closely, she realized that behind the trees that ringed the property there was a thick wall. She watched as Trent pulled up to a scanner near the gate and placed his hand on it. Within seconds, the gate began to silently swing open.

"Is it okay you're bringing me?" Victoria asked as she realized how secure the compound was.

"I okayed it with Marcus yesterday. And Justin knows you're coming. It helps that you're Eric's sister." Trent smiled at her. "And I vouched for you as well."

Trent swung the car into a parking lot and came to a stop. "Not sure how many people are here, but Justin set aside a spot for you to try shooting, if you want."

Well, she hadn't come all this way to just watch. After all, she'd sacrificed fashion in order to be properly dressed to shoot...so shoot she would.

CHAPTER SEVEN

AFTER helping her out of the car, Trent grabbed a bag from the trunk and gestured toward the largest of the three buildings in the immediate area. "That's where we're going. The other two are living quarters for the teams here for training."

Victoria heard shouts and looked toward where the noise had come from. "We're safe here?"

Trent laughed. "That's probably just a group of guys indulging in a no holds barred game of football or something. Nothing dangerous."

He opened the door of the building, and she stepped into a carpeted reception area. There was no one in the room, and Trent didn't pause as he led the way to a door to the left of where they had entered. He pressed his hand to a scanner again, and Victoria heard the door click. After pulling it open, he gestured for her to go ahead of him.

Immediately, things became more utilitarian as they stepped into a long hall. The floors were bare tile and the plain beige walls had no windows, but fluorescent lights kept the hallway from being dark. There was a smell in the air that Victoria couldn't quite place. As they neared the end of the hallway, she could hear muffled shots.

Trent opened another door with a hand scan and the noise became louder. She had kind of hoped that it might be just her and Trent there to shoot but clearly that wasn't the case.

They walked into a large room that had couches and tables and chairs scattered around it. The upper half of the wall to the left of where they'd walked in was entirely glass so she could see the range. Victoria looked at the people beyond the glass and became acutely aware of the fact that she was likely the only female in the building. She glanced up at Trent, wondering why on earth he'd brought her there.

"Hey, Hause!"

Victoria looked around to see a tall man approaching them. She recognized him from the wedding and realized that he must be Justin. He was taller than Trent by at least six inches and wore a pair of dark jeans and a black T-shirt that stretched across a very muscled chest.

"Justin." Trent shook hands with the man then touched Victoria's back as he said, "This is Victoria. She's Eric's sister."

A smile briefly crossed Justin's chiseled features. He held out his hand and took hers in a surprisingly gentle shake. "Nice to see you again. So you're wanting to do some shooting?"

"I kinda mentioned it in passing, and here we are," Victoria said with a laugh as she glanced at Trent.

"It's a good skill to have," Justin said as he crossed his arms over his chest, his feet braced apart. "Even if you're just learning for self-defense."

"And my size won't affect my ability to learn?" Victoria asked.

Justin shook his head. "We will need to adapt a few things, but once you find the right gun and get some practice under your belt, it won't matter what size you are when a bad guy crosses your path."

Victoria looked at Trent. Had he brought her there so she could learn how to defend herself? "Well, I know absolutely nothing about guns."

Another smile made a quick appearance on Justin's face. "Contrary to popular opinion, I didn't come from my mother's womb knowing how to shoot a gun either. We all had to learn at one time or another." He slapped Trent on the back. "Four years ago, this guy's main experience with a gun was in those video games he played. He's come a long way since then."

"And I have to say that shooting the real thing is much more fun than virtual guns."

"Well, let's see what you brought, Trent," Justin said as he gestured to one of the tables.

Over the next fifteen minutes, Justin and Trent had her handle a bunch of different guns to see which one would work best for her. She found it interesting that when Justin wrapped his large hands around hers to show her how to grip a gun, she felt absolutely nothing. However, when Trent moved close to show her how to hold her arm to see how the weight was, her heartbeat kicked up several notches and her cheeks warmed.

Once they settled on the gun they felt would be best for her, Justin explained the different parts of it and how it worked. Victoria really hoped they didn't give her a test because with Trent sitting so close to her, she was only picking up every other word or so.

"Let's go see how this works for you," Justin said as he pushed back from the table. He went behind a long counter and pulled out three ear protectors as well as three pairs of glasses. "And take a gander at the rules of the range before we go out."

"Safety first," Trent said as he gestured to a big sign on the wall. "Go ahead and put your ear muffs on. You'll still be able to hear us."

As she read them, she slipped the ear muffs over her head. Surprisingly enough, she heard Trent loud and clear when he said, "And these are to protect your eyes. Don't take them off while we're in the gun range."

"How are these supposed to protect my ears if I can hear you?" Victoria asked, tapping the ear covering.

Trent adjusted his own set and put on the glasses. "These are specially made to amplify ambient noises but will automatically shut off when it detects a noise above a certain decibel."

Feeling a little nervous, Victoria followed Justin with Trent behind her. She hoped that she didn't do anything stupid like shoot one of the guys or her own foot. As they walked into the area beyond the glass windows, the lighting changed. There were several divided areas, each of which had enough room for a person to stand in to shoot at a target downrange. Each one they passed was filled with a very large man until closer to the end where she noticed there were two females. No one paid them any attention as they walked.

"Here we go," Justin said as they reached the last partition.

It had a little bit more space than the others and there was no shelf like she'd seen in the pictures of gun ranges when she'd searched the night before.

Victoria sucked in a deep breath as she took the gun Justin handed her. It was all loaded and ready to go, but she wasn't sure she was. She had thought that Trent would be the one showing her how to shoot, but it was Justin who dropped to one knee beside her.

"Okay, sugar, grip it like we showed you. Firmly. You need to show the gun who's boss. Firm stance. Firm grip. And a firm pull of the trigger. Don't be afraid of it." He helped her line up her arm and her stance and then stood up and moved a step away. "Pull that trigger."

Keeping in mind what Justin had said, she gripped the gun tight in her hands, did a mental count to three and pulled the trigger. What she had been expecting—the noise— wasn't there, but the shock of the recoil vibrated up her arm.

Thankfully, she'd been expecting it and since Justin had positioned her correctly, she hadn't ended up on her butt.

"Good job!" Trent said as he approached her from the right. "How did that feel?"

Victoria looked down at the gun in her hand and then over at him. She grinned. "It felt good. Really good."

He went down on one knee beside her, an eyebrow raised. "Have I created a monster bringing you here?"

"You very well may have." She glanced down the range. "Can I try again? And maybe see if I can actually aim at and hit the target?"

"Sure thing." This time it was Trent who guided her stance—a gentle touch to her hip, to her shoulder, to her arm—and instructed her on how to aim for the target.

And once again she reacted to his presence in a way she hadn't to Justin's. Trying to focus, she closed her eyes for a moment then opened them and looked for her target. She counted to three and squeezed the trigger, relishing the sense of power it gave her. While she hit the paper this time, it was nowhere near the center that she had been aiming for.

"Justin?"

Victoria looked over to see a woman approaching them. As she neared, Victoria realized that it was Melanie. She'd only met her once at the wedding, but she recognized her right away.

"Hey, Melanie. What's up?" Justin moved away from where they were standing.

Victoria glanced at Trent and saw that his gaze was on them as Justin bent his head to listen to what Melanie was saying. Feeling that spurt of jealousy again, Victoria turned her attention back to the range. Remembering what Justin and Trent had shown her, she took up her stance, raised the gun tightly in both hands and aimed.

One. Two. Three. She pulled the trigger and stared with delight when she realized that she'd actually made it onto the black part of the target that was shaped like a man.

"Excellent!" Trent said next to her ear.

She glanced over to find him still on his knee beside her, bringing them almost eye to eye. Grinning, she prepared to shoot again. Something told her that this could become very addictive.

For the next thirty minutes, Trent stayed at her side helping her reload her weapon, giving tips and encouragement. Unfortunately, the muscles in her shoulder and upper arm were beginning to protest the unusual activity, not to mention the throbbing in her hip from all the standing. The pills she'd taken earlier had taken the edge off but pain still lingered in her hip.

"I'm gonna have to call it a day," Victoria said as she lowered her weapon.

"Muscles bothering you a bit?" Trent asked as he took the weapon from her. "You did a super job. Better than I actually thought you would."

His praise brought a flush of warmth to her cheeks. "And I enjoyed it more than I thought I would. You didn't get to shoot though."

"That's fine. This was for you." He showed her how to clean up her brass and then walked by her side back into the main room.

Justin reappeared as she pulled off the protective gear and set it on the counter.

"You picked up on that very quickly," he said as he put the gear into the cupboard. "Will we be seeing you around more frequently now?"

Victoria looked at Trent then back to Justin. "I was thinking of looking into a gun range in the city."

"There's no need if you want to shoot here," Justin said. "As long as you come with Trent or Eric, it shouldn't be a problem."

"We can talk about it later," Trent said.

Justin looked at him. "You sparring today?"

"I hadn't planned to since I brought Victoria with me."

"Maybe she'd like to hang around and see you get your butt kicked," Justin said with a wink at Victoria.

"I don't mind waiting if you want to spar, Trent," Victoria said as she wondered about the look Trent shot the other man. "It's only fair since you gave up your shooting time to help me."

"Okay, but no comments on how much stronger than me Justin is or I'll never take you shooting again."

Victoria grinned. "No comments. I promise."

Justin led the way through another hallway and up some stairs to the second floor. "This really isn't set up for spectators, but there is a bench you can sit on to watch."

The sound of physical combat reached Victoria as soon as Justin opened the door at the top of the stairs. Trent motioned for her to go ahead, and she stepped into a large open room with a high ceiling. The upper half of the walls on three sides were glass with lots of natural light flooding the room. There were weight machines, treadmills and other equipment she couldn't even begin to recognize set up along one wall as well as a couple of large areas made up of mats.

Victoria felt a little out of place with these people whose bodies moved like well-oiled machines. Her gaze went to where two guys were engaged in some kind of hand-to-hand combat. She winced at some of the blows that they landed on each other, but not a flinch showed on the faces of the men involved.

"We're just going to change," Trent said as he bent down to her. "You can go sit on that bench. I'm guessing we'll be on that mat over there."

Victoria looked to where Trent pointed and nodded. She watched as he followed Justin through a doorway beside the one they'd just entered. Feeling more than a little self-conscious, Victoria made her way to the bench. She breathed a sigh of relief at finally being able to take the weight off her throbbing hip. She'd just settled onto the bench when someone joined her.

She looked over to see a tall, dark man seated beside her, sweat running in rivulets down his neck and chest. It took her a second but then she recognized him and smiled. "Than. I didn't expect to see you here."

"I could say that right back atcha. Eric bring you?" He grabbed a towel from a stack on the bench and wiped his face and neck.

Victoria shook her head. "Trent brought me out to do some shooting and then Justin offered to show me how he kicks his butt on the mat."

Than laughed. "Justin kicks everyone's butt. Maybe I should spar with Trent. Give him a chance at coming out on top." He winked at her. "Not much of a chance but at least better than what he has with Justin."

"So, how did your date with Lindsay go?" Victoria asked, remembering the interaction between the two when they'd been up at Lucas's cabin.

Than's shoulders slumped and the smile that seemed to always be on his face slid away. "Well, I did everything she asked, and I thought it went pretty good, but she won't give me the time of day anymore."

"And that bothers you?" She tried not to grin at the forlorn look on his face. "For some reason I pegged you as happily going through life serial dating."

"That has been my preference, yes, but it's usually because most women are all too happy to talk about themselves on that first date. By the end of the evening, there's nothing left to learn about them. With Lindsay, it wasn't that way. I swear I know as much about her now as I did before the date."

"Clearly you've been dating the wrong type of woman, Than. Many of us aren't so eager to spill all our secrets on the first date."

"Have you had your first date with Trent yet?" Than asked as he quirked an eyebrow, his smile returning.

"Trent and I aren't dating." But as soon as she said the words, Trent and Justin walked into the room, dressed for their sparring session, and her mouth went dry. Though Justin definitely had the muscles and the height, Victoria found Trent's less defined—but still clearly there—muscles to be more physically attractive.

Than laughed. "Well, perhaps you should be."

Before she could respond, they were joined by Trent and Justin.

Trent scowled at Than. "What are you doing here, Miller?"

Than leaned back against the wall, stretching his legs out and crossing his arms over his chest. "Just keeping Victoria company while Justin pummels you."

"Nice," Trent muttered as he kicked Than's foot. "I'm sure when he's done with me, he'll still have plenty of energy to take care of you."

Justin thumped Trent on the back. "Let's go do this."

Victoria watched as they walked away from her. They stood close together in the middle of the mat, and though she could see that Justin was talking to Trent, she couldn't hear what he was saying.

Over the next thirty minutes, Victoria alternated between wincing and wanting to cheer. Justin would knock Trent down, but he'd immediately jump to his feet and go back for more. She could hear Justin calling out short instructions to him and even Than got in on the action a time or two, shouting out encouragement to Trent.

Finally, after about thirty minutes, Justin sent Trent sprawling to the mat and this time he stayed there, spread-eagle on his back. He lifted his hand and dropped it onto the mat. It must have been a signal of some kind because Justin walked over to where he lay and held out a hand to help him to his feet. They stood talking again for a minute before Justin slapped him on the shoulder, and they headed back to the changing rooms.

"I'm surprised he can move after that," Victoria commented as she watched Trent disappear through the doorway.

"We're subjected to it often enough that we get used to the pummeling Justin hands out. In all honesty, Trent does better against Justin than I do." The corner of Than's mouth lifted in a wry grin. "Every time Justin knocks me down, I get mad and come up swinging. He just sends me right back to the mat because I'm letting my emotions dictate my moves. Trent is better about keeping that under control."

Victoria thought of the run-in they'd had with the pack of teenage boys at the theater and now knew that even in the midst of anger, Trent would have been able to take them on. Even though he often came across as easygoing, she was beginning to sense that he kept a tight control on himself and there were parts of him that ran deeper than she had ever imagined.

She had to admit, the rather flippant, lighthearted persona she'd seen over the past couple of years had been attractive on one level, but she had needed more. Seeing that he did, in fact, have more depth than she'd realized, Victoria knew that she was in danger of losing her heart more than she'd ever been before. And she wasn't sure how to protect herself from that happening.

CHAPTER EIGHT

THOUGH normally after a beating like that from Justin, Trent would have lingered under the heat of the water, he spent just enough time to soap away the sweat. Knowing that Victoria was waiting, he dried off and dressed quickly. He downed a couple of pills to help with the pain that was already settling into his muscles. The last thing he wanted to do was limp his way through the rest of the evening with Victoria.

After making sure his hair wasn't plastered to his head, Trent grabbed his bag and the bottle of water he'd taken from the fridge and left the changing room. He spotted Justin standing with Than and Victoria. Justin hadn't taken the time to change so was no doubt planning to inflict pain on someone else before he retired to his apartment in the living quarters.

Though he did have a home in the city, Justin seemed to spend most of his time at the compound and the apartment he had there. Trent wasn't sure why. Justin was a man of few words when it came to himself. He didn't talk a whole lot unless it was related to the training he did. More often than not, he stood or sat in silence with his arms crossed over his chest, his expression totally unreadable. Trent knew he'd never ever play poker against the man. Actually, he wouldn't play poker against any of the guys at BlackThorpe. They'd all been trained to guard their reactions.

"Ready to go?" Trent asked Victoria as he joined them.

She smiled up at him. "Yep. And I hope you're hungry after all that."

"Oh, no worries there. I could eat a horse."

"Ah. Sorry. No horse on the menu tonight."

"She's feeding you?" Than asked, curiosity on his face. One corner of his mouth lifted as humor sparked in his eyes. "I'm hungry, too."

"I have plenty," Victoria said, a little too eagerly for Trent's liking. "You're welcome to join us."

"Sounds great. What's your address?"

Trent tried not to see red as she rattled it off for Than. This wasn't how he'd imagined the evening unfolding. Oh, he hadn't been looking at it as a date, but he'd hoped that as they spent time together she'd perhaps come to see him in a different light. More than just her brother's goofy friend. Having Than around was definitely going to put a crimp in that plan.

Trent shot the guy a look that should have warned him off, but all the idiot did was grin at him. With a sigh, he shifted his bag to his other hand. He shook Justin's hand but ignored Than altogether before following Victoria to the door.

"I can't believe you're still walking after that session with Justin," she said as he pushed open the door for her. "You were amazing."

A bit of the frustration that had taken up residence in his body eased at her words. "Amazing? I got beat up."

"Yeah, but you kept getting back on your feet. Admirable is getting knocked down but not giving up."

Trent tried not to take too much pleasure in her words. "Well, Justin was holding back. He holds it back for most of us since we're not on his level or even close to it."

"He seems like a pretty intense individual. I wouldn't want to get on his bad side."

"No worries there. I'm not sure you could get on anyone's bad side." Trent smiled as he led the way into the reception area and held the door open to exit the building. The sun warmed him as they walked to where he'd parked the car. He put his bag on the back seat and retrieved the stool for Victoria.

"So you think you'd be interested in doing more shooting?" Trent asked a few minutes later as he guided the car through the gate and out onto the road. He hadn't anticipated how much she'd get into it when he'd suggested she come with him to the range.

"Definitely. I just need to get myself a gun and find a range."

"You already have a gun," Trent said with a glance at her.

Her eyes widened. "I do?"

"Sure. The one you were shooting with is yours."

"Really?" A smile spread across her face as she reached out to touch his arm. "Thank you!"

"I didn't know if you'd really enjoy it, but since you seem to have a real knack for shooting, there's no reason you should stop." Keeping his gaze on the road, he said, "If you want, we could make it a weekly thing. I'm out here pretty much every Saturday afternoon anyway. You might as well tag along and do some shooting of your own."

Victoria was silent for a moment then said, "I might take you up on that."

"Just give me a call by Saturday morning to let me know if you want to go. It's no problem to swing by and pick you up since you're pretty much right on my way."

"I might not be able to go every week, but I'd really like to continue. It ended up being a lot more fun than I thought."

He heard her phone chirp, and she reached into her purse to pull it out. They lapsed into silence as she had a text conversation with someone. Trent was hoping his own phone would signal a text message from Than letting him know he really wasn't coming, but no such luck.

When they pulled into Victoria's driveway, she said, "Guess we're going to have more company for dinner."

"We are?" Trent said as he turned off the ignition.

"Yeah. That was Alicia. I invited her to join us since Than is coming. The more, the merrier at this point."

Trent wasn't sure he agreed with her, but it might be nice to have someone else to entertain Than. He got the stool for Victoria and then returned it to the trunk of her car when she was through with it. As he shut the trunk, he wondered if she'd order one for his car if he asked. Or would she find that too presumptuous?

Entering the house felt a bit too much like coming home. Even stepping into his own apartment hadn't brought this depth of feeling. The spicy tomato aroma along with the faint scent of fresh bread caused his stomach to growl. Trying to keep from drooling, Trent followed Victoria to the kitchen and watched as she got up on a stool to check the crock pot. Steam rose when she lifted the lid to stir it.

"Smells delicious," Trent commented as he leaned a hip against the counter.

She gave him a quick smile before returning the lid to the pot. "I hope it tastes as good."

"What can I do to help?"

"Well, you aren't supposed to be helping with these meals at all, but since I'm going to have to make more noodles than originally planned, I'll let you put the water in the pot and put it on the stove."

Trent picked up the pot she indicated and went to the sink to fill it. When it was filled to Victoria's satisfaction, he lifted it onto the burner of the stove. She climbed her stool to add some oil and salt.

"Can you turn the burner on?" she asked. "Medium-high until it boils."

Though he wasn't much of a cook himself, Trent found he enjoyed being in the kitchen with Victoria. Of course, he'd probably enjoy being pretty much anywhere with her.

The doorbell chimed a few minutes later, and Victoria asked him if he'd get it. Anticipating it would be either Than or Alicia, Trent was a little surprised to find Eric, Staci and Sarah on the porch.

Eric had obviously recognized his car because he didn't look too surprised. Or happy. He lifted a dark brow as he said, "Uh, hey, bud. Is Victoria around?"

"Yep. She's in the kitchen." Trent stepped back to let them in. It looked like it was going to be a full-on dinner party at this rate.

Eric let Staci and Sarah precede him into the house, and they headed right for the kitchen. Trent shut the door behind his friend then turned to find him blocking his way.

Hands on his hips, legs braced, Eric said, "Something you want to tell me?"

"Not really. But if you insist, Victoria agreed to cook me some dinners in exchange for the computer system. And we spent some time at the compound shooting today."

Eric's eyes widened. "You taught my sister—my *little* sister—how to shoot a gun?"

Trent mirrored his friend's stance and nodded. "She's a natural. Just ask Justin."

Before Eric could say anything, the doorbell rang. Trent spun around and opened it to find Alicia waiting.

"Hi Trent," she said as she stepped into the house. He saw her pause when her gaze landed on her brother. "I didn't know you were going to be here too, Eric."

Eric smiled at her as he relaxed his shoulders and moved to the side to let her past. "Surprises all around today." The doorbell went again. "And apparently it's Grand Central Station here this evening."

This time it was Than, and he gave Trent a mocking smile as he stepped inside. "Well hey, Eric. Good to see you, man."

"What are you doing here?" Eric asked as he shook Than's hand.

"I ran into Trent and Victoria at the compound and was invited to come for dinner."

Trent scowled at him. "He kind of invited himself."

"Well, it appears that I'm not the only one," Than said with a nod in Eric's direction.

"We were actually going to take Victoria out for supper, but this smells so much better than anything we likely would have gotten at a restaurant."

Trent followed Eric and Than as they also headed toward the kitchen. His gaze met Victoria's, and she gave a quick shrug with a rueful smile. With Staci and Alicia there, it appeared Victoria didn't need his help anymore.

"Why don't you guys go to the living room?" Victoria suggested as she handed Alicia a basket of apples. "I think we have this under control."

Trent reluctantly left the kitchen area and led the way to the living room where he sat on the couch that faced the dining room and kitchen.

"So why don't you tell me about this shooting lesson you gave Victoria?" Eric said as he sat down across from him. "I had no idea she was even interested in learning."

"I happened to mention that I had a gun—well, that all of us BlackThorpe guys did actually—when we were at the theater the other night. She said that she wished she could learn to shoot. I contacted Justin and Marcus and got permission to take her out to the compound to give it a whirl."

"Give it a whirl? She's barely four feet tall, if that, and you're giving her guns to play with?"

Trent scowled at him. "Geez, Eric, she's a small adult, not a child. It's not like I handed her a Glock or an Uzi and let her go to it. Justin helped me find a gun that was light enough for her and fit her grip. She did great. And she enjoyed herself so I think, all in all, it was a good thing for her."

"Sorry, but I just have a hard time thinking about Tori with a gun."

"Well, you'd better get used to it. I plan to encourage her to get a permit to carry concealed once she's had more practice."

Eric's eyebrows shot up. "What? Why would you do that?"

"You do realize how vulnerable she is, right?" In a low voice, Trent explained what had happened after the movie when the others had already left. "I don't want anyone to ever think they can take advantage of her because of her size. So...I'm giving her the tools to protect herself. I don't expect her to shoot anyone, but if someone should break in here or really threaten her, she'll have a chance at protecting herself."

Eric regarded him with a narrowed gaze before finally saying, "Okay. I'm going to accept that you have Tori's best interests at heart, but is there something more? I mean, I know you've kind of had something for her, but is she finally reciprocating?"

Trent debated what to say. This was her brother, after all. "Nothing's changed. She's happy with us being friends."

Than gave a shake of his head. "Tsk. Friend-zoned. You poor man."

"I guess you'd know how it feels since you've been friend-zoned more times than I can count," Trent said with a smirk.

Than sighed. "Women!"

"Or maybe it's just one woman in particular?" Eric suggested.

Ignoring the question, Than turned the conversation in the direction of work. It wasn't too much longer before Sarah came bolting over to tell them supper was ready.

At Victoria's direction, they each found seats around the table. Trent was rather surprised when she told him to take the seat next to her. He figured she would have put as much distance between them as possible, particularly with her family there. Maybe he was making some progress after all.

True to Victoria's word, the meal was as delicious as it had smelled. There was plenty for everyone, though if Victoria had hoped to have leftovers, she was going to be out of luck. When she finished off the meal with fresh-from-the-oven apple crisp with vanilla ice cream, Trent figured he'd died and gone to heaven.

Once the meal was over, they all pitched in to clear the table and load the dishwasher. Not long after the cleanup was done, Eric and Staci decided to leave.

"See you tomorrow," Eric said to Trent as he followed his wife and daughter out the front door. "Thanks for supper, Tori."

"Anytime," she called after them before closing the door.

Thankfully, Than didn't seem inclined to stay much longer after Eric left, and Alicia followed a short time later.

When it was finally just the two of them, Victoria said, "I hope you didn't mind having to share your home-cooked meal."

He did, but he wasn't going to tell her that. "It turned out fine. The meal was excellent."

She gave him a quick smile. "It was a good thing I made so much. I'd planned to freeze some, but guess I'll just need to make more."

Though he wanted to hang around, Trent knew it was time he took his leave as well. He didn't want to push things. "I'd better head out, too."

"Thank you," Victoria said as they stood up.

Trent glanced over at her. "For what?"

Her expression was serious as she regarded him. "For listening to me. For hearing me say I wanted to do something and instead of finding reasons why it wouldn't work, you made it happen. That means an awful lot to me."

Trent swallowed past the tightness in his throat. "You'll never know if you can or can't do something unless you try at least once."

Victoria nodded. "I understand there will be some things that I won't be able to do, but I want to at least try the ones that are possible before dismissing them. Or having them dismissed for me."

"Well, I'm game for anything, so let me know if there's something else you want to try," Trent said.

Victoria grinned. "It's nice to have someone willing to try these things with me instead of trying to talk me out of them."

"Well, hopefully your family doesn't get too upset with me. Eric wasn't exactly thrilled when he found out I took you shooting."

She shrugged. "He'll get over it. I *am* an adult, after all. These are choices I get to make because of that."

"Exactly."

As they approached the door, Trent felt a touch on his arm. He turned to look down at Victoria. She lifted her arm toward him and he bent down, surprised to feel her hand on his shoulder as she brushed a kiss across his cheek. "Good night."

Feeling more hopeful than he had in a while, Trent couldn't wipe the grin off his face as he walked to his car. Obviously she was happier moving at a slower speed. He could do that. As long as the outcome was in his favor. Their favor.

Trent resisted the urge to call Victoria on Sunday. Now that she was actually letting him into her life, he wasn't going to push it. He just hoped that she'd call soon to let him know she wanted to go shooting on Saturday. But in the meantime, he needed to get through a busy week.

By the time Friday rolled around, he was beat. He and his team had been working on a new security program for a client, but testing had proven it to be too vulnerable. That result had required that they spend long hours figuring out how best to shore up the defenses for the special needs the client had.

Once work was done on Friday, Trent stopped at a restaurant not far from his place and picked up a pizza. All he wanted to do was eat, veg in front of the television for a bit and go to sleep. And he hoped he woke to a call Saturday morning from Victoria saying she wanted to go to the range with him.

Trent took the pizza and a bottle of soda into his bedroom. He tossed the box onto the bed and changed into a pair of shorts and a muscle shirt. Flipping through the channels, he managed to polish off his first piece and then settled in to watch a movie he'd found and ate a few more.

A blaring alarm brutally dragged Trent from sleep. Disoriented by the jarring noise, he lay for a second trying to figure out what was going on. Then his brain kicked in, and he leaped from the bed, struggling to free his legs from the sheets and stay on his feet.

Heart pounding, he raced for his computer. He hit the button to turn on his monitor, impatiently waiting for the screen to come to life. As soon as it was on, he began to type in commands. His phone began to ring, and he wasted precious seconds to retrieve it from the nightstand beside his bed.

"What's going on, Trent?" Marcus's deep voice rumbled in his ear.

"The system is under attack. Someone is trying to hack into the BlackThorpe network."

"Can you stop them?"

Trent appreciated Marcus's calm voice even as his heart was nearly pounding right out of his chest. "I think so, but I really need to get into the office."

"Can you call one of your guys to monitor it while you get to the office?"

"Yes. I'll get Ethan on it."

"I'll meet you there."

The line went dead, but Trent didn't move the phone from his ear as he continued to frantically type commands into his system. He activated the voice command on the phone. "Call Ethan."

Within seconds, the phone was ringing.

"'ello?" Ethan's groggy voice came on the line.

"Ethan. Wake up. The network is under attack. I need you to get to BlackThorpe so you can monitor it there while I drive in."

There was a moment of silence then Trent heard the rustle of sheets and the murmur of voices. "I'll leave right away."

"Call me when you get there. Get logged in immediately so I can head out. I can't leave this unsupervised while I drive in. And I think we might need to sever the network connection if we can't head them off soon."

"Understood," Ethan said before the line went dead.

After putting his phoned down, Trent stayed bent over his keyboard, staring at the data that streamed on his monitor. His blood was pumping, and he wanted to physically do something, but all he could do was sit there, watching the information that scrolled on his screen. The best security program around protected BlackThorpe's network. He and his guys had written it themselves. And they'd tested it over and over. The defenses were in layers around the system, and no two defense layers were the same. Getting through the outer one just meant there were several more to go.

Unfortunately, this person had already breached the first defense shortly after the alarm. The alarm was set to go off at the first sign that someone was attempting to hack the system. So having the time between when the alarm sounded and the first breach be so short concerned Trent. Big time.

CHAPTER NINE

A KERNEL of fear sprang to life in him. This was his job on the line. He'd told Marcus that the defenses they'd put in place were impenetrable. Had they been wrong?

Trent took several deep breaths, willing Ethan to call and let him know he'd arrived. He needed to get to the office. As he waited, he put in his ear piece so that he could move and talk at the same time.

It seemed to take an eternity before Ethan called.

"Okay, I'm heading out now." Trent jumped up from his chair. "Stay on the line with me and tell me what's going on while I drive."

He grabbed a pair of jeans and a T-shirt and shoved his feet into his shoes without putting on socks. After scooping up his wallet, phone, laptop bag and ID, he bolted out of his apartment and went down to the underground parking garage in his building. Everything seemed to take twice as long, and he prayed the cops didn't pull him over as he tested the speed limits on the way.

Finally, he parked in his assigned spot beneath the BlackThorpe building. With Ethan still talking in his ear, he took the elevator to the floor where the computer hub was located. He immediately spotted Marcus and Alex when he stepped out of the elevator.

"What's going on, Trent?" Alex asked as he approached where they stood watching Ethan work.

With a sick feeling in his gut, Trent could tell from the information scrolling on the big monitor on the wall that the hacker had breached the second level of security.

Trent shook his head. "I'm not sure, but whoever this guy is, he's good."

"You are good, too," Marcus said, his tone firm and confident. "How can you stop him?"

He glanced over at his boss where he stood, a dark figure. He wore black pants and a black T-shirt, and it looked like he hadn't even been in bed when the alarm went. It was one o'clock in the morning, the man should at least look a *little* frazzled.

Trent turned back to Ethan. "Do you recognize any of this? Sometimes these hackers have a style or a signature that you can pick up on. None of this looks familiar to me though."

"Me, either," Ethan said as he continued to type commands.

Trent sat down at a station beside him. If the hacker managed to breach the third protocol they had in place, he would need to pull the plug. It was the worst case scenario since it meant that their overseas teams—well, anyone outside the building actually—wouldn't have access to the information stored on the network. But it was a failsafe that would sever the hacker's connection with their system. It wasn't ideal, but it was the lesser of two evils.

For the next half hour, Trent and Ethan worked side by side, sharing observations and watching as the attack continued. Sweat slid down the side of Trent's face as he watched this unprecedented attempt on their system. He tried to tamp it down, but fear pooled in the pit of his stomach. There was a lot at stake if this attack was successful. The confidential information stored on their servers could mean death for certain individuals if it got into the hands of the wrong people.

He felt a hand on his shoulder and glanced up. Marcus stood behind him, his expression as stoic as ever. "You've got this. Breathe. Take a second to clear your mind and then focus on it again."

Closing his eyes, Trent took a deep breath and let it out. He *could* do this. Marcus had hired him because he was one of the best in the business. *Please, God, open my eyes to see what I might be missing in this. Help me to see how to protect the information that needs to be kept safe. Give me Your wisdom to do this. I can't do it on my own.*

He opened his eyes, took one more deep breath and let it out in a huff. Then he focused once again on the monitor before them. Fear was still there, but it was being overshadowed by the determination to show this hacker that he and his team at BlackThorpe were not to be messed with.

"See if you can find him, Ethan," Trent said as he watched code change on the screen. "Let's see if we can beat this guy at his own game."

"We really need Tracer for that. He's the best person to track him down."

"Then get him on the phone and tell him to haul his butt in here." Trent felt Marcus's hand leave his shoulder as if the man realized he no longer needed to offer his physical support.

The gleam in Tracer's eyes, when he walked into the computer center thirty minutes later, was all Trent needed to see. The lanky man had earned his nickname by being able to trace computer signals like no one else. He wasn't sure how Marcus had done it, but somehow BlackThorpe had managed to swipe Tracer right from under the government's nose.

"Trace this guy, man. We need to find him."

Tracer sat down at his computer and shoved a pair of horn-rimmed glasses onto his angular face. "Will do, boss."

Satisfied that Tracer had a handle on that, Trent turned his attention back to the monitor. He felt better knowing that they were no longer just on the defensive. With Tracer on the hunt, they had just gone on the offensive. He had complete confidence in his team and even if Tracer couldn't get a lock on the guy, whoever the hacker was would know that they were looking for him. Maybe that would make him think twice about trying again.

Marcus and Alex stayed with them through the early morning hours. They had sent out emails to all the employees worldwide to let them know that they were not to attempt to access the BlackThorpe network until further notice. Around nine o'clock, the attack abruptly stopped without the hacker having been able to pierce the third layer of defense.

"Did you find him?" Trent asked as he shot a look at Tracer.

"No." The one word was heavily laced with frustration.

"Close?"

"Very. If he'd stayed online even just two or three more minutes, I would have had him. He knew it, too. That's why he disconnected the way he did." Tracer thumped his desk with his fist. "So close."

Trent slumped back in his chair. All the tension that had coiled in his body over the past eight hours seemed to evaporate, leaving him exhausted. But there would be no time for resting. They had to repair the damage done to the network and analyze the code the hacker had been utilizing to dismantle their defenses.

He stood up and stretched from side to side. Ethan and Tracer also stood to work out the kinks in their bodies.

"Why don't you guys hit the showers," Alex said. "I'll get you some breakfast."

Trent hoped that a shower might help to rejuvenate him. Going on just two hours of sleep in the last twenty-four, particularly after such an adrenalin rush, was clouding his brain.

"We're going to call in the rest of the admin team to alert them to what has transpired," Marcus said as he walked with Trent to the elevator. "We'll meet in the boardroom."

The gym and showers were on the second floor, so Marcus said he'd catch the elevator on the way back up and let Trent and Ethan in first. Tracer had stayed to monitor the system until one of them got back. They rode in silence to the lower floor. Trent had no doubt that Ethan was trying to sort through the events of the past few hours as he was.

"Meet back at the computers when you're done," Trent said as they entered the gym.

Alex and Tracer were the only ones in the computer room when Trent returned, but he knew Ethan would be right behind him. Nothing more had happened in the time they'd been gone.

"All quiet on the monitor front," Alex said, pushing up from the chair he'd been sitting in as he watched the screens. "There's breakfast over there for you guys."

"Thanks, man," Trent said as he went to pour himself some coffee. He wasn't a huge fan of the beverage but right then he needed the caffeine. His mouth watered a bit at the sight of the breakfast sandwiches on the tray as well.

Tracer headed for the showers once Ethan returned. Trent sat sipping his coffee and staring at the large monitor that sat still now where not that long ago it had been streaming with code. It was going to be a long day as they dissected and analyzed that code.

"Marcus said the meeting will be at eleven. Will that work for you?" Alex asked as he stood with his cup of coffee in hand.

Trent glanced at the clock on the wall. "Yeah, that should be fine."

"I'll see you then." Alex left the three of them in the dimly lit computer room.

After Ethan and Tracer had gotten some coffee and food, Trent sat down with them around the conference table they had in the room. Over the next forty-five minutes, they laid out a plan of defense as well as one of attack. And made sure that the computers were being physically monitored twenty-four seven throughout the rest of the weekend.

Trent told Ethan he could go home since they had called in one of the other team members, but he refused. When *both* of the other guys on the team showed up, Trent knew they were as anxious as he was to figure out what had happened and who was behind the attack.

Just before eleven, he took the elevator to the floor where the admin team would be meeting. Everyone was already in the boardroom when he walked in.

Marcus didn't waste any time starting the meeting and bringing everyone up to date. Trent could see the tension on all their faces. No doubt it matched what was on his. They never took an attack on the company lightly. And he figured they were likely wondering—as he was—if this attack had anything to do with what Eric had gone through earlier in the year.

When his phone rang mid-way through the meeting, Trent winced. He'd forgotten to turn the ringer off. Figuring it was one of the guys, he almost tapped the screen without looking, but then the name on the display caught his attention. *Victoria.* He groaned inwardly and did the only thing he could right then and tapped the icon that would send the call right to his voice mail. He hated to do that to her, but he just couldn't take her call in the middle of this meeting.

Trent turned off the ringer on his phone then quickly tapped out a message to Victoria.

Sorry. In a meeting. Won't be going to compound today. Something has come up.

He'd have to call her later and explain in a little more detail. Preferably when he didn't have an audience.

He glanced up to find all sets of eyes on him. "Sorry." Lowering the phone to his lap, he turned his attention back to Marcus.

When the phone vibrated in his hand a minute later, he dropped his gaze to read the message on the screen.

Okay.

His heart sank as he wondered if he'd just undone everything he'd managed to build with Victoria in the past couple of weeks. But it couldn't be helped. He slid the phone into his pocket. He needed to put that aside so he could focus on what he needed to tell the guys about all that had transpired since the alarm had first blared out its warning ten hours ago.

When the meeting wrapped up an hour later, Eric went with him to the computer room.

"You need to get some rest," he said as they walked to where Ethan and Tracer were working with the other guys on the team.

"Can't do that yet." He had hoped to call Victoria but with Eric hanging around, he put it off.

The other two guys—Max and Nick—were at their stations now. He knew that Ethan and Tracer had likely brought them up to speed on what had happened, but now they needed to formulate a plan of attack as a complete team.

"Let's huddle up, guys," Trent said as he poured more coffee into his cup and laced it heavily with sugar and cream. "You going to stick around for this, Eric?"

"I would, but I have a feeling your conversation is going to go beyond my level of understanding pretty quickly. Give me a call later."

Alone with his guys, Trent slumped into a chair. As he glanced around the table, he could see the exhaustion on

Tracer and Ethan's faces, but their eyes still shone with the challenge of what they faced.

Victoria stared down at her phone again. The message from Trent had been weird. She knew enough to realize that he'd sent her straight to his voicemail. His text had come pretty quickly after that so it seemed that he hadn't even taken the time to check his messages. Not that she'd left one.

She had planned to make supper for him again and had even started it already by the time she called to tell him she wanted to go with him to the range. Now she had a whole crockpot full of chicken and sauce and no idea if she'd be eating it on her own. She'd also made a batch of buns and used some of the dough to make cinnamon rolls that she'd intended to send home with him. His loss.

Since she'd cleared her day to spend it at the range with Trent, it took her a little while to focus in on something to do. She'd done all her chores earlier in the morning because she'd wanted the house clean when they got back from the range. She had a bit of paperwork to do for the company, but that didn't take much time.

Finally, she filled a large glass with some lemonade she'd made earlier and went out to the chaise lawn chair in the backyard and settled down to read for a while. The summer afternoon was warm and filled with the sounds of the neighborhood. She set her tablet in her lap and leaned back in the chair. It was times like this she was glad she lived in a house instead of an apartment. She loved spending time in her yard. The large trees cast dappled shadows across the grass, and when the breeze kicked up, the rustling of the leaves soothed her.

Summer was her favorite season followed by spring and fall. Winter was definitely the season she liked the least. The cold months made her joints hurt more than they did in the summer. Plus, they had never really been a winter sports type family. She'd never learned to ice skate or ski. And now, as an adult, she had no interest in learning.

Even though she was a bit disappointed at not being able to go shooting, Victoria let out a sigh of contentment as she lifted her tablet and pulled up the book she'd been reading over the past few days. It wasn't how she'd planned to spend her afternoon, but it wasn't a bad alternative.

CHAPTER TEN

TRENT'S head throbbed, and his eyes were crossing from looking at code for so many hours. Marcus had made sure they had plenty of food as they worked and the hours had ticked by quickly. But he was coming up on forty-five hours with only two hours of sleep. And by the time he looked at the clock, it was too late to call Victoria. It would have to wait until the next day.

They'd managed to fix the damage to the network's defenses and had even added an additional layer based on what they'd learned about the hacker from analyzing his coding. But continuing on much longer without sleep would most likely result in him missing things or making mistakes that they couldn't afford at that point.

"Why don't you guys head for home?" Matt suggested. "Nick and I can handle this through the night. Just come spell us off in the morning. Right, Nick?"

The other computer tech nodded. "If anything pops up again, we'll let you know right away."

Trent thought about just making use of the apartment in the building, but the thought of falling into his own bed was definitely appealing. "Okay. But call if anything looks the least bit suspicious."

Ethan and Tracer went down to the garage with him. They made the trip in silence. Trent didn't doubt that the other two guys were as tired as he was. He was just grateful to have such a great team of men working for him.

"Thanks for all your help," Trent said as they reached his car. "Get some rest."

Ethan nodded. "You, too."

After finding himself almost falling asleep on the way home, Trent didn't bother with a shower. He set his alarm for seven and fell into his bed.

When his alarm went off the next morning, he lay in bed for a bit longer trying to wake up completely. The seven hours he'd gotten hadn't been enough. He reached for his phone and called the guys at the office. After being assured everything was under control, he decided to take the shower he'd skipped the night before. He wanted to phone Victoria but figured he should wait until after he was ready to go to the office so his call wouldn't wake her up.

By seven forty-five, he was showered and dressed. As he sat on the edge of his unmade bed, he tapped the screen to call her. It rang several times before he heard the line open between them. She didn't say anything right away, but he could hear movement on the other end so just waited.

"Hello?" Her voice sounded husky from sleep.

"Hey, Victoria. It's Trent."

"Trent? What time is it?"

"Almost eight. I'm sorry to call so early, but I wanted to make sure I touched base with you."

He heard more movement and tried not to picture her in bed. It was a place his thoughts did not need to go.

"What's going on? Are you okay?"

"I'm fine. We just had a bad hacking attempt at BlackThorpe early Saturday morning. I've been tied up dealing with that and then cleaning up the mess afterward. I'm actually heading back into the office now to monitor things for the day." He rubbed his forehead. "I'm sorry I couldn't take your call yesterday. It came right in the middle of a meeting with Marcus, Alex and the rest of the group."

"I'm sorry you've had to deal with that."

Trent sighed. "Yeah. It's been a stressful couple of days. Hopefully, things will be back to normal by the end of today."

"Well, thank you for letting me know what happened."

"I'm sorry we couldn't get to the range, but there's always next week."

"Yep."

"I hate to run, but I've got to get back to the office. They sent me home to get a few hours of sleep, but I need to get back to relieve the other guys now."

"Have a good day," she said, her voice soft.

"Thanks. You, too." He wanted to prolong the conversation, but other responsibilities called to him. After saying goodbye, he pulled on his socks and shoes and grabbed his work bag and headed out the door.

Victoria usually slept until eight thirty on Sunday mornings, so she stayed in bed a bit longer after Trent had hung up. She was glad he'd called. After not hearing from him the previous day, she'd begun to wonder what was going on. For a brief moment, she'd considered calling Eric to see if he knew what was up but had decided to just wait until Trent contacted her.

She was still trying to figure out how things were between her and Trent. Unfortunately, it seemed he'd slipped into friend-mode since the night he'd come to set up her computer. Though there was still some teasing and joking, the flirting was basically gone. It was like he'd decided he no longer wanted that after having spent more time with her.

But then, he *was* still willing to spend time together. Between the home-cooked meals and the offer to take her to the range, he certainly wasn't cutting their contact. But, on the other hand, he also wasn't making much contact between their times together on the weekends.

With a groan, Victoria rolled out of bed. She was going to give herself a brain cramp trying to figure it out. Pushing those thoughts out of her mind for the time being, she went to the bathroom to get ready for church.

Victoria was a bit disappointed—but not really surprised—that it was another week before she heard from Trent. He called her on Friday night to see if she wanted to go to the range the next day.

"I was thinking about it," she said.

"Well, if you do want to go, we're going to have to head out a little earlier. I need to be back in the city by five."

She guessed that meant their dinner was out. "We don't have to go. If you have other stuff to do, I don't mind waiting for another time."

Trent sighed. "Are you sure? I hate that even though I offered to take you, I haven't been able to for two weeks in a row now."

"Not to mention that I still owe you a few more dinners."

"No worries there. I do plan to collect...eventually."

"So we'll just plan for a trip to the range another time," Victoria said, trying to ignore the disappointment that filled her. She was beginning to think that she'd missed her chance with Trent. All those times of brushing aside his flirting had finally sunk in with him, and now when her interest was piqued, his had waned.

"Thanks for understanding." The line sounded muffled like he'd covered the phone to talk to someone then he came back on the line. "I gotta run. Take care of yourself."

"You, too." Victoria lowered the phone from her ear when the call disconnected and stared at it. There was no reason she should feel hurt. She had no one to blame but herself for the way things were now. She'd come to see the depth in Trent too late. The things that attracted her to him were things he hadn't shown her in the first few years they'd known each other. Not that she'd given him much chance. Her fault for that, too.

Trent sighed as his chin dropped to his chest. After the week he'd had, this was the last thing he'd needed.

"Seriously, Trent, why do you live in such a sparse apartment? I mean, you have nothing here. You could afford the best, and yet you live like this."

Though he tried to tune out his sister's whining, it just wasn't working. Trent pushed up from the armchair and turned to face her.

"I live like this because I *want* to. I don't need a fancy space. I have everything that meets my needs here."

"Well, if I had known how you lived, I would have made reservations at a hotel."

"You still can," Trent pointed out.

Tiffany Hause-Ashbury wrinkled her nose at him. He wasn't sure, but Trent thought maybe she'd had some work done since he'd last seen her. Most likely a nose job. Her hair and makeup were expertly done. Perfection was her goal in life. She was very much like their mother in that regard.

He wished that she had gone the hotel route since having her at the apartment meant giving up his bed for the next couple of nights. After the stressful week he'd had, his plan had been to order in, watch a movie and sleep until he felt human again. And if Victoria phoned to say she wanted to go shooting, he would have gladly gone.

Now everything good about his weekend had just been torpedoed by the unexpected arrival of his sister and her expectation that he would be her plus one at the wedding she was in town to attend.

"Why didn't you let me know sooner that you were coming?" Trent asked as he went to the fridge and pulled out a bottle of soda. "Getting a call this morning that you were arriving this afternoon was a little short notice."

Tiffany's lips tightened briefly. "It was a last-minute decision."

"Yeah, I'm not buying that. This wedding would have required you to send in your RSVP months ago. What's going on?" He settled back into the armchair and watched as his sister perched on the edge of his couch, slowly crossing her legs. He wondered if she ever just slumped comfortably anywhere.

"Fine. Andrew was supposed to have accompanied me to this wedding. He decided at the last minute not to come."

"Trouble in paradise?" They'd only been married for two or three years. He couldn't remember exactly.

"No. Something else came up that demanded his attention." She didn't meet his gaze, so Trent decided not to press.

It still didn't make him happy that his weekend got trashed all because his brother-in-law decided to be a no-show at the wedding.

"Take me out for dinner, Trent." She gave him a beguiling smile. "I'm hungry."

Trent sighed. Her idea of going out for dinner and his were two different things. Anything that met her standards was going to mean going through a drive-through on the way home to get something that actually had substance. But she was his sister and he did love her—even if she was a bit of a handful—so he would take her to dinner. And try not to think about the home-cooked meal he *could* have been enjoying instead.

By the time Trent got back to his apartment early Sunday afternoon, he was surprised he had any hair left. Life with a high maintenance woman was definitely not his thing. It had been an endless flow of complaints. His towels weren't soft enough. His pillows weren't fluffy enough. His car wasn't a luxury model. He should have worn a tux instead of just a suit. And the list had gone on and on…

When he'd finally waved goodbye to Tiffany that morning as she'd boarded her flight, he'd had a new understanding of why Andrew may have decided to decline to accompany his wife. No doubt the guy had spent the weekend lounging around, belching and eating greasy fast food.

He stripped the sheets off his bed, since they now smelled a bit too much like his sister's perfume, and stuffed them into the washer. After that was taken care of, he grabbed the bag containing the burger and fries he'd stopped for and dropped down on the couch. With the remote in one hand and a burger in the other, Trent was back in bachelor heaven.

But once the burger and fries were gone, he flipped mindlessly through the channels. After contemplating it for a few minutes, he grabbed his phone and tapped the screen to call Victoria.

"I'm heading out to the compound for some shooting and sparring. You want to come along?" he asked when she answered the phone.

There was a beat of silence before she said, "Sure. What time were you planning to go?"

"I just have to get my stuff together."

"Okay. I'm on my way home. I'll see you there in a bit."

Feeling like his weekend was finally taking a turn for the better, Trent packed a bag with his workout clothes and the weapons. After switching his sheets to the dryer, he left the apartment, a sense of anticipation filling him.

Victoria hurried into the house as fast as she could on her crutches to change. She'd gone out to lunch with Alicia and her folks after the service, so she was still wearing her church clothes. She would have liked to have had a bit more time to pick something to wear but knowing that Trent could arrive at any minute kept her from lingering too long.

In the end, she settled on a pair of black capris and a light blue T-shirt. She ran a quick brush through her hair and changed her earrings from the hoops she'd been wearing to a pair of studs. Since she still hadn't heard the doorbell, Victoria took the time to freshen up her makeup.

She had been a bit surprised by his call. She'd figured that since their Saturday plan to go to the compound had been canceled, she wouldn't hear from him again until the next weekend. It seemed that while they spent time together on the weekends, during the week he had other things that grabbed his attention.

After a quick debate, Victoria pulled out the container of frozen chicken from the week before. She put it on the counter to defrost while they were gone. Though he hadn't mentioned dinner afterward, she'd be prepared if he did say something. If not, well, she had food for a couple of nights for herself.

The doorbell rang as she was putting on her shoes. She finished tying them, grabbed her purse and went to answer the door. Trent stood there, a broad grin on his face. Her heart skipped a beat at the sight of him. He wore a pair of cargo shorts and a T-shirt, both in black, which give him a bit of an edgy, dangerous look. Not really a look she'd associated with him before, but it worked on him.

"Ready to go?" he asked.

"Yep." She hesitated then grabbed her crutches before she stepped from the house and locked the door.

"Pop your trunk?" Trent called to her as he walked down the porch steps.

Using her key fob, she did as he requested and then followed him down the steps. He was waiting with her stool beside the car by the time she got there.

His brows drew together as he watched her come toward him. "What happened?"

When she came to a stop next to him, she lifted a crutch. "These?" At his nod, she said, "My hip has been giving me some problems lately. Particularly if I have to walk any distance."

"Have you been using them for a while? I've never seen them before."

Victoria was beginning to wish she'd left them behind and had just endured the pain. He was looking at her different now, she was sure of it.

"I've been using them for a few months now but only when I was on my own. Unfortunately, I'm having to be even more careful now so I don't do more damage to the hip."

It looked like he had more questions, but instead he nodded and stepped back so she could use the stool to get into the car. Suddenly, the joy of going shooting with him slipped away. Maybe he wouldn't have asked her to come along if he'd known about the crutches. And he was no doubt counting his blessings that he'd stopped pursuing a relationship with her.

During the drive, Victoria half expected him to ask her more questions about it, but instead, he focused on the issues they'd had at work. She'd heard a bit about the incident from Eric, as well as high praise for Trent and his team.

Despite the sadness that had taken up residence in her heart, Victoria enjoyed hearing about his work. It was clearly something that he took very seriously and did very well.

"So how was your week?" Trent asked. "Anything exciting happen?"

"Nothing too spectacular. Certainly nothing on the level of your excitement."

"Well, weeks like this are few and far between, and for that I'm very grateful."

"I did receive an email about providing some of our products to a local store. It sells accessibility products and is just starting up. I'm meeting with the guy this week to see what he's looking for and to show him some of our stuff."

"That's great." He sent her a quick grin. "You could end up supplying products on an ongoing basis for him, right?"

"That would be ideal," Victoria said, happy that the questions he had decided to ask her weren't about her hip.

"Where exactly do you get your products from?"

"My dad designed most of them with a little input from me, and we work with a company overseas to manufacture them. It's sort of a ministry outreach as well. The company we work with has a high standard for its treatment of the people who work there. We wanted to make sure of that before we partnered with anyone. It would have been nice to have them made locally, but it would have made the cost prohibitive for individuals and companies alike. So the next best thing was doing what we could to ensure that those making the products were treated well."

"You hear a lot about the substandard working conditions overseas," Trent commented as he turned off the highway.

"Yes, which is why we wanted to make sure we weren't contributing to that. The company we work with often employs both the husband and wife and provides care for any children they have. We fly over periodically to make sure they continue to provide for their employees the way they said they would. So far, it's been working well."

"Is this something you foresee doing long-term?" Trent asked as he pulled up to the gate and lowered his window.

Victoria didn't answer right away. In truth, it wasn't. It had been mainly due to her dad's work to help adapt things for her that they had come up with the idea of providing them on a larger scale. She would have actually preferred a job that wasn't tied into her dwarfism. Not that she wanted to pretend that side of her didn't exist, but she wanted a chance to focus on other interests that were equally important. Even if she wasn't sure exactly what those were. "Until something better comes along, I will assume that this is where God wants me."

"What else would you consider doing if not this?" Trent swung the vehicle into a parking spot and came to a stop.

"No clue."

Trent came around to open her door and help her out. "Well, if you keep improving your shooting, you could consider something that involves guns."

Victoria laughed. "I'm sure that would thrill my family. None of them are exactly pleased that I've taken up this particular activity. Well, except for Brooke. She thinks it's cool."

"Are they opposed to guns? I guess I never thought to ask before suggesting we go shooting."

Victoria glanced up at him as they walked toward the front door, Trent keeping his pace slow. "No, but it wouldn't have mattered. I don't need their permission to do something like this. I think they'd like me to, but the reality is, I'm an adult now and quite capable of making my own decisions."

He opened the door for her and smiled. "That's for good and sure."

Victoria felt a lot more comfortable moving through the hallways of the building than she had the last time. This time around she knew what lay ahead and was looking forward to it.

"Thought we might have scared you off," Justin said when they walked into the main room.

"Not a chance," Victoria assured him. "I'm just getting warmed up."

"It can be rather addictive." A quick smile crossed Justin's face but then his brows drew together. "Although I'm not sure how it will work to shoot with your crutches."

"I won't use them when shooting. I just need them when I'm walking to lessen the movement of the hip. Standing in one place for a little while shouldn't be a problem."

"Alright then, let's get you some gear."

CHAPTER ELEVEN

THIS time around, Trent stayed with her for about ten minutes, going over the basics once again. Victoria thought she remembered most of it but was glad for the refresher. Once she showed him she remembered what she was doing, he left her alone, apparently planning to do some shooting of his own.

He was in the section next to her so she paused for a few minutes to watch him shoot. For someone who spent most his days behind a desk, he was surprisingly adept at shooting. His cluster of shots was way tighter than hers. She discovered then that she had a strong competitive streak. She wanted to do as well as he did. Maybe even better. His height and her lack thereof didn't come into play when shooting. She liked the level playing field.

After about thirty minutes of shooting, they cleaned up their brass and left the shooting range area. Victoria was pleased that her arms didn't hurt as much this time when she finished, and even the pain in her hip was just a dull ache. She knew her arms would most likely still be sore the next day, but maybe not as sore as last time.

"You ready for some sparring?" Justin asked as he took their safety gear.

"If you've got the time," Trent said as he finished putting away the guns. "And if Victoria's okay with hanging around."

"Sure. I don't have anything planned for this afternoon."

As before, she went with the guys to the gym and found a place to sit on the bench while she waited for them to reappear. This time, Than didn't show up to keep her company, so she pulled her phone out while she waited. She was texting a message to Alicia when the guys came back out.

Victoria paused mid-text to watch as they took up their positions on the mat. Once again, Trent and Justin had a brief conversation before they began their session. Making a mental note to ask Trent about it later, she looked back down at her phone to finish the text to Alicia. She felt movement on the bench next to her and looked over, half expecting to see Than there again but instead it was a young woman.

She wore workout clothes that fit her body like a second skin. The tank top she wore showed clearly the muscled definition of her arms and shoulders. Her tanned skin served to highlight the light blonde hair that was pulled back in a long ponytail.

When she glanced over and saw Victoria watching her, she smiled. "Hi, I'm AJ."

"I'm Victoria."

AJ nodded her head toward the mat where Trent and Justin were now engaged in physical combat. "I know Justin, but do you know who the other guy is?"

"Yes. That's Trent Hause."

A small smile curved the corners of the woman's mouth as her gaze returned to the sparring duo. Victoria looked back at the guys as well, trying to ignore the pit in her stomach. Who was this woman? She must be with one of the training teams that came to the compound since she knew who Justin was.

"Do you know if he has a girlfriend?"

Ugh. Victoria just wanted to ignore the woman *and* her question. Then she was tempted to lie and say *yes,* but she couldn't do that either. "Not that I know of."

AJ glanced at her. "Are you friends with him?"

"Yes. He and my brother work with Justin at BlackThorpe."

The woman slid her hands under her thighs and leaned forward slightly. "Would you introduce me to him?"

Seriously?

Victoria wondered what it was like to have such confidence to approach a total stranger just because they liked what they saw. Well, technically the woman had approached her first. Clearly, she didn't see her as a threat. AJ hadn't asked if *she* was Trent's girlfriend. She'd just asked if he had *a* girlfriend.

"I suppose." She turned her attention back to the guys and hoped that the woman would just stop talking.

Her phone vibrated, and she looked down to see a response from Alicia. Needing a place to vent, she tapped out an account of what had just happened. After sending it, she leaned back against the wall and watched as Trent rushed Justin and the two of them went down in a scramble of arms and legs. They didn't stay down though. Both popped back up to their feet and began to circle each other again.

Too bad Than wasn't around. Maybe he could have taken AJ's attention from Trent. Victoria's spirits had risen during the drive out and their time shooting, but now they plunged back down. And it was going to get worse. Trent and Justin ended their session and headed in their direction.

As they got closer, Victoria saw Trent's gaze go to AJ. Fighting a *yuck* feeling in her stomach, she stayed seated even as AJ stood. There was just no need to reinforce the differences between them.

"Hey, AJ," Justin said. "How's it going?"

"Good. You guys were doing great out there."

AJ looked at her, and Victoria let out a sigh, but thankfully, before she could say anything, Justin beat her to the punch.

Justin gestured to AJ. "Trent, this is AJ. She's part of the team in from Washington for the month. AJ, Trent. He heads up the virtual security division for BlackThorpe."

"Computers? Nice. Another important arm of security for sure." She smiled at him, and Victoria fought the urge to kick her in the shin. "You're in pretty good shape for a guy with a desk job."

Trent's brows drew together briefly. "BlackThorpe impresses on us the importance of staying in shape. And Justin makes sure that we don't forget."

"He definitely is a tough taskmaster."

When Trent looked at her, Victoria hoped she had a pleasant expression on her face. She also hoped she had managed to keep every other emotion from her eyes when their gazes met. There was no reading the expression in his.

"I'll just go get changed, and we can leave."

Though it was clear that they were leaving together, it didn't stop AJ from making her move.

As Trent turned to go, AJ rested her hand on his arm. "Hey. Any chance you'd be interested in going for a drink?"

Trent's gaze shot to Justin then back to AJ. "Uh, no. I don't drink."

AJ shrugged but was apparently undeterred. "Maybe dinner then?"

"I appreciate the invitation, but I'm afraid I must decline." He gave her a quick smile before turning and heading to the changing room, but Justin stayed behind.

"I thought you said he didn't have a girlfriend," AJ said as she turned to Victoria, a frown on her face.

"He doesn't."

"So is he gay?"

Victoria had to laugh at that one. "No, he's not."

Justin cleared his throat. "AJ, just because a man doesn't fall at your feet doesn't mean he's gay or unavailable. You're just not Trent's type."

Surprise crossed AJ's face as if she had never even considered that option. She turned on her heel and walked away.

Justin's gaze met hers and even though he didn't full-on smile, Victoria could see the humor in his eyes as he winked at her. "But I do believe *you* are."

Warmth rose in her cheeks, and she couldn't keep a smile from turning up the corners of her mouth. She felt much better by the time Trent returned. He looked relieved to find it was just her and Justin at the bench.

"Thanks again, man," Trent said as he gripped the hand Justin held out. "Not sure why I feel like I should thank you for tossing me around, but I do."

Justin slapped him on the back. "It's always a good idea to be polite to someone who can beat you up." He smiled at Victoria. "Hope to see you again. You're improving quite rapidly."

"Thanks. I really enjoy it, so I'll be back soon."

Neither of them said much as they made their way out of the building to the car.

"So, that was a bit odd," Trent said as he drove through the open gates of the compound.

"What's that?"

He glanced at her. "AJ asking me out like that."

"Hey, we girls are taught that we don't have to wait for the guy to make the first move anymore. She really took that lesson to heart, apparently."

"Did you talk with her?"

"A little. She seemed more interested in watching you spar with Justin."

"Why would I be interested in going out with someone who's only here for a month?"

Was that the only reason he'd declined her invitation? "Maybe she was just looking for a little entertainment while she was here."

"Well, I'm not into that type of thing."

"Also, long distance relationships aren't exactly an anomaly these days. Maybe she was thinking along those lines."

Trent shook his head. "Doesn't matter. I'm not interested in either of those sorts of relationships. Or her, for that matter." He paused. "What I don't understand is why she assumed that I was available, especially when you were there."

Victoria laughed. "Really? I'm sure that it never even crossed her mind that we might be together. She didn't ask if I *was* your girlfriend. She asked if you *had* a girlfriend. I told her no."

Trent's brows drew together as he shot her a look. "First of all, you could have just fudged that a little to spare me that embarrassing encounter. And second, why would you think people wouldn't assume we were together?"

"Just society's perceptions." Victoria suddenly wished this conversation would just go away. She paused but when he didn't respond, she continued. "You can't tell me you're unaware of them. When two people who are so noticeably different associate, society often just assumes they wouldn't be together in a romantic way. It's not just a little person and an average-size person. You get it with a mixed race couple, too. People are more likely to assume they're just friends, not romantically involved. Not that they don't accept them as a couple once they realize there is a connection there, but it's usually not their first assumption unless there is something obvious to connect them. If you'd been a little person sparring, and I was there watching, I'm sure she would have automatically assumed a romantic connection even if we were just friends."

Trent kept his gaze on the road, but she could see that his jaw was tight. "I suppose you're right about society's perception, but it still doesn't make it right."

"It's happened with me, Staci and Sarah, too. If the three of us are out together, no one assumes that Sarah is Staci's. They assume she's mine. Even if Staci is holding her. Most the time, it's not meant with malice. I honestly think AJ would have held more malicious thoughts about me if I'd lied and said I was your girlfriend. She didn't see me as a threat for your attention, so she just dismissed me."

Victoria sensed an undercurrent of anger coming from Trent but couldn't quite figure out the reason. Was he upset she'd offered him up to AJ? Did he wish she'd identified herself as his girlfriend? Or did her explanation of society's view upset him?

Whatever it was, the remainder of the trip was made in silence, and Victoria knew she'd be eating the food she pulled out of the freezer by herself. He hadn't said anything about dinner and with his current mood, she wasn't about to offer. In reality, she needed some time to think about what had transpired at the gym, too. The yucky feeling still lingered in her gut even though Trent had turned down AJ's invitation.

It had been just one more reason she'd resisted Trent's attempts to get her to go out on a date with him. It wasn't just that he was an average-size guy, but that he was an *attractive* average-size guy. She hadn't wanted everyone to look at them and wonder why—of all the women he could have had in the world—he'd settled for her.

"Thank you for taking me again," Victoria said as she climbed down from the car.

"You're welcome." Trent returned the stool to her car then said, "Have a good week. I hope your meeting goes well."

"Thanks." Victoria watched as he walked around to the driver's side of his car and got in. As he began to back out of her driveway, she turned on her crutches and headed for the house.

She took off her shoes and dropped her purse on the table on her way to the living room. Victoria went to the couch and settled on it with a sigh, sliding the crutches off her arms.

This was too confusing with Trent. His anger made no sense. He was the one who'd backed off from his pursuit of her. She figured they had settled into a friendship of sorts. If he was interested in more, wouldn't he be in contact with her more than just once a week?

Victoria rubbed her forehead then leaned her head against the back of the couch. A certain sense of dissatisfaction had been building inside her of late. Her life was so predictable and—if she were totally honest—a bit boring. That was probably why she'd been so excited about going to the range and cooking dinners for Trent. It was something that took her out of the monotony that had engulfed her life.

Monday mornings her mom would be there at ten o'clock to take her grocery shopping. They'd come home and unpack them then go out for lunch. Sometimes Brooke joined them. Usually one day a week she had Sarah over to do some baking and to spend time with her. One or two times a month she met with a group of other little people. And she usually tried to attend the weekly women's Bible study at church. The rest of her time was split between running her business, spending time with family and taking care of her house.

Trent's question about whether she saw herself continuing the business long term had gotten her thinking. And keeping with the honesty theme, she had to admit that she really didn't want to continue with it long term. She'd just kind of fallen into it when her dad had created some unique things that they thought other little people might be able to make use of. It had kind of just grown from there, though it still wasn't a huge business. She and her dad could handle most of it with the help of a friend who took care of things like marketing.

But Victoria really wanted to have something more— something different—in her life. What that was, she didn't know yet, but there had to be something that would give her a sense of fulfillment and purpose.

She leaned down on the pillow at the end of the couch and lifted her legs, wincing as her hip protested the movement. But maybe she had to deal with the hip surgery first and then look at some sort of change in her life.

And she wondered what was going to happen with Trent. Her heart hurt at the thought that what had transpired earlier might have killed their budding friendship. She wished she understood men better because maybe she'd get why Trent had backed away from the flirting and seemed content with just friendship. Had spending one-on-one time with her made him realize that maybe friendship was what he wanted? Or had it been that he'd finally accepted that *she* didn't want anything more?

Except that now she did. But just as it had been fear that had kept her from letting him get too close over the past couple of years, it would be fear that kept her from going after him now.

Trent fought the urge to fling his bag across the room when he got to his apartment. But since it contained firearms—one of which was loaded—he set it down with care on his table. He grabbed a drink and then sat down in front of his computer. Ever since the attack, he'd found himself monitoring things more than he had before. But even that couldn't calm the turmoil within him.

He wasn't even sure what he was most upset about. The fact that Victoria had been in pain and using crutches for some time, and she hadn't told him. Not only that, she'd hidden it as if she couldn't trust him with that information.

It also stung that she'd willingly offered up his single status to that woman without even a hesitation. Was she not feeling any sort of connection with him the way he was with her? And then her revelation of society's perceptions had made him mad. Is that why she'd resisted his earlier attempts at a relationship? She didn't want to be subject to society's perceptions of them?

He certainly didn't give a rip what society thought about anything. And his sister could no doubt vouch for that after her most recent stay with him. She'd made sure he knew—

once again—every single thing that was expected of him because of who he was. The son of a rich family. Though he'd been raised hearing lectures about it, he'd chosen not to follow his family's idea of how society should operate. Their perception of society that elevated them above others. The guides by which he lived came from his belief in God and how the Bible laid out he should live his life.

Maturity and his own experiences had moved him past the point of looking at just the surface of people. He wasn't ignorant, but sometimes he forgot that a good chunk of the world either didn't care to embrace those who were different or they outright rejected them. Those were the ones who seemed to be at the forefront of Victoria's own perceptions of the world.

Would he be able to get Victoria to set aside any fears she had about how people might look at them in order to give a relationship a shot? That was assuming she felt anything for him. Some days he felt a growing confidence that she did but then days like today left him wondering.

If some guy had come up and asked him if she had a boyfriend, he would definitely have figured out a way to make it clear to the guy that she was unavailable.

As he sat there, once again thinking about Victoria's comments on society, he realized that his own family might have some difficulty accepting her. Not that that would ever stop him from being with her if she was willing. But would they see in her the things he did? Her strength. Her loving heart. Her sense of humor. Even the whole thing with the guns had shown him again how determined and strong she was. She hadn't let her size hold her back from at least trying to learn to shoot.

But why did it seem that she would let her size hold her back from a relationship with him? Maybe it was time to just come clean with his feelings and ask her to give him a shot.

No jokes. No flirting. Just feelings.

This was where his own inexperience with women worked against him. He hadn't dated at all in high school, and though he'd had a couple of relationships in his early twenties, he hadn't been able to picture a long-term future with either of the women. So yeah, he had very little experience from which to draw on when dealing with Victoria. And he couldn't exactly go to his best friend to ask for advice. Than could probably have given him some pointers, but they likely wouldn't have been anything that would lead to a long-term relationship.

So he was left to try and figure it out for himself, all the while hoping he didn't do anything that would scare her off. It was the hardest thing in the world to not pick up the phone every single night to talk to her. To ask her how her day had gone and share about his. But if his lighthearted attempts at flirting with her every couple of weeks had scared her off, he could only imagine what daily calls from him would do. For all he knew, the main reason she spent time with him was because he was giving her the opportunity to do something she really wanted to do.

He gave his head a shake. It shouldn't be this complicated. He'd thought giving her a chance to really get to know him was the right course of action. But it seemed like all that had happened was that he'd ended up with a new friend. A good friend, no doubt, but still just a friend.

All he wanted was to have a simple, straightforward conversation with her.

Hey, I really like you. Want to go out on a date?

And hopefully, she'd reply just as straightforwardly.

Sure. I really like you, too. What time are you picking me up?

But no, he'd been convinced that he could tease and flirt his way into her heart. Then when that hadn't been successful and he'd been handed another chance with her needing his help, he still hadn't been able to make it work. Or at least he didn't think he had.

CHAPTER TWELVE

WITH Victoria was sending out so many mixed signals, Trent really had no idea either way. Bottom line, if he was truly honest with himself, he was too scared to just put it right out there. He clearly had his own set of fears. The biggest one being that if he pushed her too soon, she'd shut him right down. Permanently. So far, even with some of the mixed signals, there were enough positive ones that he hoped he still had a chance.

With a frustrated sigh, Trent pushed back from the computer. Other guys might turn to sports when aggravated, but his go-to was his video games. It had been quite a while since he'd played any of them so it took a few minutes to find the one he wanted and to get it set up. But at least it would give him a couple hours of mindless entertainment.

Victoria left her meeting with the man who'd wanted to purchase her products feeling encouraged. She'd still not heard back on the hotel proposal she'd sent out a few weeks ago, so it felt good to be moving in a positive direction with this. It had been invigorating to see his dedication to helping little people and others who had disabilities that meant they faced some of the same challenges as someone with dwarfism. It definitely was his passion in a way it had never been hers. But it had been infectious nonetheless.

And it had been nice to not have her thoughts dominated by Trent for a couple of hours. But now as she walked to her car, Victoria realized that the person she wanted to call first to share about the meeting was Trent. But he hadn't told her to call him to let him know, he'd just said he hoped it went well.

Victoria allowed herself to wallow in her frustration for the duration of the drive home, but once inside the house, she forced herself to push it aside. She had some numbers to work up and then she needed to put some serious thought into her future.

And maybe what she was going to do about Trent.

When Eric had stopped by his office earlier to invite him to a family barbecue, Trent had jumped at it. Not just because the food at the McKinleys was always terrific, but it gave him an opportunity to hang around Victoria. It would also offer him a chance to judge how she might be feeling toward him after the previous weekend's fiasco.

As he pulled to a stop in front of the McKinley house, Trent noticed that Victoria's car wasn't there. Hoping that maybe she'd caught a ride with Alicia or Brooke, he bypassed the front door and headed to the gate that led to the backyard. He did a quick scan of the people there and noticed immediately that Victoria wasn't among them.

Maybe she was just late.

"Hey, Trent," Eric called from where he stood next to the barbecue.

Trent veered in his friend's direction, the smells from the grill drawing him like a magnet. His stomach rumbled appreciatively in anticipation of having its best meal all week.

"Where's Victoria?" Though he hadn't planned to ask about her, he just couldn't help it.

Eric gave him a quick look as he opened the grill and began to turn the meat. "She's on a date."

The words were like a kick to his stomach. They robbed him of breath, but he worked to get the words out because he wasn't sure he'd heard right. "A date?"

"Uh, yeah." Eric slowly lowered the lid back down. "When Mom told me that, I assumed the two of you must have come to some sort of understanding and were just staying friends. But I'm guessing maybe that wasn't the case?"

Trent swallowed hard, hoping the pain in his heart was not visible on his face. "To be honest, we never really talked seriously about a relationship between the two of us."

Eric tilted his head. "You guys have been spending a lot of time together, and yet you never got around to talking about the two of you? What was going through your mind, buddy?"

"I was thinking that I didn't want to pressure her. That I wanted her to spend some time with me without all the stuff of the past few months. I had hoped that she'd come to feel something for me like I do for her. Guess that kind of backfired on me, huh?"

Eric's brows drew together. "I'm not sure what to say, man. Why didn't you just ask her out?"

"I *did*. Several times. She shot me down each time, but it was never an angry *don't ever ask me again* type of refusal. I kinda figured she just had some reservations about me because she's a little person and I'm not. That's why when I had the opportunity to spend some time with her because of the computer issue and then going to the gun range, I jumped at it. I thought it would give her a chance to get to know me a little more, and maybe it would help her push past those reservations to give us a shot."

"Maybe this isn't a date." Eric shrugged. "You know how Mom gets when a guy comes around her daughters. And now that she doesn't have Brooke to worry about, she's focusing on Victoria and even Alicia."

Trent shoved his hands into the cargo pants he wore. He stared blankly at the grill, wondering if he'd really lost his chance with Victoria. The food that had smelled so enticing just minutes ago now turned his stomach.

"Don't give up yet, dude. You've got one thing this other guy hasn't."

Trent glanced at him. "And what's that?"

Eric grinned and lifted an eyebrow. "Big brother's stamp of approval."

"Yeah, something tells me that doesn't exactly rank high on Victoria's list of things a guy should have."

Eric chuckled, but for once Trent didn't join him. "Yeah, you're probably right about that."

Doug McKinley appeared then with a platter of hot dogs. "Let's add these in, son." He glanced at Trent. "How you doing, young man?"

"I'm doing fine, sir." And now he was lying to his best friend's dad. "And you?"

"Doing well. Doing well." He set the empty platter down on the table beside the grill. "So I hear you've been teaching my baby girl how to shoot a gun."

"Actually, Justin was the one who did most the teaching. And she's quite a natural at shooting. Picked it up really quickly."

The older man smiled. "That's my girl. She mentioned how much she enjoyed it and that she appreciated you taking her to practice."

"Well, that's what friends are for," Trent said, choking a bit on the word *friends*.

Doug sent him an unreadable glance. "Well, I appreciate you looking out for my girl."

"I'm not sure she'd agree with you on that. She seems to feel she doesn't need anyone looking out for her."

Eric's father grinned. "You do know her well. But hey, I'm her father. I'm allowed to look out for her. And I appreciate anyone who also does so."

"Are you ready over there?" Caroline McKinley asked from where she and the other women were seated.

"Nearly," Doug called back to his wife.

Caroline and Brooke stood and went to the house, disappearing into the kitchen. They quickly reappeared with several bowls on trays.

"Hey!"

Trent heard Danny's shout and turned to see Lucas walk into the backyard. The man caught his nephew in a tight hug when he tackled him, then he made a beeline to where Brooke stood. Lucas reached out to snag her around the waist and draw her close. Trent watched in envy as Brooke's arms crept around Lucas's waist and she lifted her face for his kiss.

Trent let out a sigh. If Victoria wasn't the woman for him, he could only trust that God had someone better in mind. He couldn't think who that might be, but for now he needed to just put aside his hurting heart and deal with it later.

When the family gathered to pray, he stood next to Danny and bowed his head. There was no mention of Victoria as they ate, which was probably a good thing. He noticed Alicia watching him off and on and wondered if Victoria had confided anything in her about the times they'd spent together.

They had just finished the meal when Doug's phone chirped. He pulled the phone from his pocket and looked at the message before standing up. "Be back in a bit."

Trent watched as he walked to the gate and swung it open. His heart clenched and his stomach heaved when he saw Victoria walk through the gate with a man not too much taller than her. So, she had ended up choosing a man closer to her own height. Though she'd said it wasn't something she used to determine whether or not to date someone, it was apparent that, in this case, the shorter man had won.

Doug shook hands with the man and then motioned to the back door. Without coming over to the group, the three of them disappeared inside. Trent sat for a moment, not unaware of the silence that had just descended over the group.

Was he strong enough to stay and watch Victoria with her new boyfriend?

Absolutely not.

He glanced at Eric and then stood up, his gaze going to Mrs. McKinley. "Thanks so much for dinner, but I've gotta run."

"Don't you want dessert?" Caroline asked, her brow furrowed.

"Very tempting, but I'll have to take a rain check on that."

Turning back to Eric, he said, "See you at church on Sunday."

He tried not to look like he was running as he walked quickly to the gate, but he needed to be out of there before the trio reappeared. He couldn't quite figure out why Doug would have taken them into the house without introducing the new guy to the rest of the family, but as he strode along the driveway to where he'd parked, he decided it didn't matter. Victoria had made her choice and it wasn't him, so what she did was no longer his concern.

If he'd been a drinking man, he likely would have headed to the nearest bar to drown his sorrows. Instead, he decided he would go home and immerse himself in a virtual world where he could kill things and vent his hurt and anger.

"Wasn't Trent here?" Victoria asked as she approached the table where the family sat. Seeing the curious looks on their faces, she said, "Oh, sorry, this is Dan Stanridge. Dan, this is my mom, Caroline. And that's my brother Eric, his wife Staci, my sister Brooke, her boyfriend Lucas and my sister Alicia."

No doubt he wouldn't remember all their names, but he'd come to know them soon enough. As he shook hands with each of them, Victoria looked back at Eric. "Trent?"

"He had to leave," Eric said curtly.

Victoria frowned. She had hoped to be able to talk to him for a little bit. So much was happening in her life, and for the first time she felt like she was in control and moving it in the direction she wanted to go.

"Dan is going to be my new partner in TASC," her dad announced as he sat down beside his wife. "Victoria has decided she wants to focus on some other things, so Dan is going to buy her out."

"Really?" Eric said as he looked at her, his brows drawn together. "I didn't know you wanted out of the company."

Victoria shrugged. "The last few weeks I've been thinking more about what I want to do with my life. The company has been good, but it's Dad who has been the driving force behind it. It's his inventions that have really made it what it is. I think he and Dan will work well together. They're both passionate about it in a way that I haven't really been in the last couple of years. Plus, the money from the sale of the company will allow me to finally get the surgery on my other hip."

"Is that the main reason you're selling your portion in the company?" Lucas asked.

Victoria was a bit surprised to hear him join the conversation. He was usually a man of few words. "Not really. It definitely has played a part in it, but there's a lot more, too."

"Well, don't use the money from the sale of the company for your surgery. I'll take care of that."

Victoria stared at him in shock. It was easy to forget that Lucas was basically made of money. He never flashed it around though he had been generous in allowing the family to make use of things like his cabin. "I couldn't take that. But thank you for offering."

A smile spread across Lucas's face as he slid an arm around Brooke's shoulders. "What good is it to have money if you can't use it to help people out? Especially when those people are important to the woman I love."

Victoria blinked back tears as she looked at her sister and saw her nodding.

"Tori, take the offer. You deserve it." Brooke smiled. "I know it's hard to accept such a large gift of money—ask Lucas how many times we've argued about it—but, in this case, I agree with him."

"I don't know what to say. If you're sure..."

"I wouldn't have offered if I wasn't sure," Lucas said. "Just send me the information and I'll have it taken care of."

If she hadn't already been feeling overwhelmed by all the things that had transpired lately, Lucas's offer would have pushed her over the top. Tears flooded her eyes as she went to give Lucas a hug and then Brooke. "Thank you. I know that's not enough...but, just thank you."

Lucas smiled at her, his gaze warm. "It gives me joy to be able to do this for you. We'll get the ball rolling on this as quickly as I can so you can get on the road to recovery."

Her heart was almost bursting with joy over everything. Her dinner with Dan had gone well as they'd discussed things regarding the sale of the company. And spending time with him had also reinforced a few other things in her heart and mind. And now Lucas had agreed to cover the cost of her surgery.

If only Trent were there to share in the joy, it would be perfect. She was sure he would be happy for her, too.

For the first time in a long time, Victoria found herself excited about life and what was to come. She still hadn't decided exactly what she was going to do when she was no longer working for the company. But now that she didn't have to use the money for her surgery, she had a little bit more breathing room to figure it out.

She just wished that Trent had hung around long enough for her to tell him about it. But she'd already planned to call him the next day to see about going to the range. And hopefully he'd agree to dinner so she could share it all with him. Her heart skipped a beat at the thought of spending time with him again. It seemed like forever since they had talked.

"Well, I promised Victoria some cheesecake to finish off our celebration of the sale," Dan said. "So if you'll excuse us, we should probably head out."

"Give me a call, sweetheart," her mom said as she pressed a kiss to her cheek.

"I will."

She and Dan made their way to his car and then to the restaurant that he'd promised her had served fantastic cheesecake. He was right, but by that point, she was ready to go home. It had been a long day, and she wanted to make sure she was in bed at a decent hour so she was ready to go out with Trent the next day.

The ringing of his phone woke Trent the next morning. He groaned and rolled over to reach for it. But he came up with air as he slid onto the floor. It took a second for him to orientate himself as the phone rang again.

He grabbed it from the coffee table and moved his thumb across the screen, hoping it was in the right place to accept the call. His head hurt, and it was easier to keep his eyes closed.

Pressing the phone to his ear as he leaned back against the couch, he said, "Hello?"

The word came out more abruptly than he'd planned, but the pulsing pain behind his eyes was distracting him. When there was no response, he cleared his throat and repeated his greeting.

"Trent?"

Trent sighed. Well, at least if he was dreaming, the headache would go away as soon as he woke up.

"Trent? Are you there? What's wrong?"

Maybe this wasn't a dream. "Victoria?"

"Yes."

"Why are you calling me?" As soon as he said the words, Trent wished he could take them back. It was what had passed through his mind, but he shouldn't have said them. In spite of everything, he did still consider her a friend and once he got over the heartache, he hoped they could continue to be friends.

Maybe.

"I, uh, was just calling to see if you were going to go shooting today. If so, I'd like to go as well."

Shooting? He could only imagine what that would do to his head. And what spending time with *her* would do to his heart. "Sorry, I'm not going today. I'm not feeling well."

"Oh no. Can I do anything for you?"

The concern in her voice was almost his undoing. He almost gave in to her offer. Almost. "No. I'm sure I'll feel better once I've had some sleep." His head would anyway.

"Okay. I'm sorry if I woke you."

"No problem. Have a good day."

"You, too. Hope you feel better."

"Thanks." And then the conversation was over.

Trent leaned his head back against the seat of the couch. Even though nothing he'd drunk had been alcoholic, he felt like he'd really tied one on. The headache was no doubt due to him having spent almost twelve hours playing video games, drinking soda and then falling asleep at an odd angle on the couch.

It had been a stupid, stupid thing to do. If the alarm had gone off for another hacking attempt, he would have been in no shape to handle it. He was a grown man and needed to pull himself together.

Sure, the pain in his heart hurt more than he could ever have imagined, but he still needed to make sure he could function. And somehow he needed to figure out how to keep the pain from flooding him every time he saw Victoria and her new guy. In the McKinley family, he'd found what he'd missed out on for so many years of his life, and Trent hated to think he would have to give them all up if he couldn't get past this pain. He could still hang with Eric away from the family if worse came to worst, but he wanted to keep them all.

Gripping the phone in his hand, he pushed to his feet and moved toward his bedroom. He dropped the phone on his nightstand and went to the bathroom. He downed some painkillers, stood in the shower letting the hot water beat down on his sore neck and shoulders before falling into bed. The pain pills had taken the edge off his headache, and exhaustion still pulled at him since he'd only had about three hours sleep when Victoria had called.

He prayed sleep would come quickly so he could get past this period of weakness and get back to life as an adult.

CHAPTER THIRTEEN

VICTORIA was disappointed that Trent hadn't been up to going to the range, but more than that, she was worried about him. He hadn't sounded like himself when she'd called and then hearing he wasn't feeling well had immediately brought her concern. She wished he'd let her do something for him, but understood why he hadn't agreed to that.

She sighed as she climbed onto a stool at the counter and stared at the preparations she'd been working on before phoning Trent. Supper was once again underway in the crockpot. From now on, she was going to wait for definite confirmation before starting a dinner for him. Twice now, she'd jumped the gun.

Frowning, Victoria's thoughts went to the previous night. Something didn't add up and that worried her. She'd never known Trent to not at least acknowledge her presence if they were at the same event. But he'd left her folks' place the night before without even saying hi or goodbye. And then—in addition to just sounding bad—he had been almost curt with her. She supposed if he wasn't feeling well that would make sense. She knew from experience that sometimes she was more abrupt with people when she was dealing with pain. Hopefully that was all it was.

But what if it wasn't?

After a somewhat restless night, Victoria gathered all her medical information and sent it to Lucas. She was thankful for how God had provided a way for her to get this surgery without having to deplete her savings. It had been hard not to view it as a handout, but the reality was, she'd been praying and trusting God to provide the money she needed for it. She'd thought the sale of the business had been His answer, but it was almost as if He'd given her that to test her. To see if she would still be thankful even knowing that paying for the surgery out of the sale money would leave her with very little for the future. And in seeing that she had, indeed, been thankful, He'd provided in such a way that her financial future was a bit more secure.

Victoria just wished she could share the news with Trent. Even if he'd changed his mind about being interested in her romantically, she still considered him a friend. And she wanted to share this blessing with him.

Her doctor had warned her that once things were in place financially, he would make sure the surgery happened quickly. That wasn't surprising since he hadn't been happy with her putting off the surgery as long as she had. With that in mind, she spent the next few days getting things in order. Though she'd been through it before with her other hip and knew what to expect, she still found herself fighting a case of nerves. Surgery was surgery. It always held a risk, and she couldn't put that thought from her mind, though she tried to not let it overwhelm her.

She knew her whole family would be praying for her and that in itself was a comfort. But when the call came on Thursday that her surgery would be the next Monday, Victoria's worry kicked up a level. She'd had no idea that things would move *that* quickly. Lucas must have pulled some strings along with getting the ball rolling. In addition to calling her about the date, the doctor wanted her to have some blood tests done before the surgery so she'd had to make time for that in her day.

On Friday night, the family gathered at her folks' place once again, but this time Trent wasn't present. Victoria didn't know if he hadn't been invited or if he'd declined the invitation.

"No Trent tagging along tonight?" she asked when Eric sat down next to her at the table.

"Nope. He and Than have been in Denver most the week doing an onsite evaluation for a company. They're supposed to get back tomorrow afternoon, I think."

Victoria was relieved to hear that it wasn't him avoiding her that had kept him away from the family dinner, though she still wasn't sure what was going on with him. She'd been so tempted to text him the night before to let him know about her surgery date, but something had held her back. Their last few interactions had been...off, and until she knew why, she didn't feel comfortable reaching out to him like that.

"You didn't have to go with them?" she asked.

Eric shook his head and lifted Sarah onto his lap when she approached them. "This was more in line with what Than does than me." He looked at her, his expression serious. "You ready for the surgery?"

"As ready as I'll ever be. At least, since I've been through this before, I know what to expect."

Eric nodded. "Well, you be sure and let us know if you need any help."

"Mom's going to stay with me for the first couple of weeks, I think. Last time it was too difficult at their place because of the stairs."

"She'll take good care of you. I think she misses having us more reliant on her."

"Yeah, I think so, too. And I'm glad she's willing to put her life on hold for a little bit."

"Guess shooting will be put on hold for a bit as well," Eric said.

Victoria nodded. Though she wasn't sure there would have been shooting anyway given how things seemed to be with Trent at the moment. "But once I'm healed up from the surgery, shooting will be even better. Do you get out to the range much?"

"Not as much as Trent does, but I do try and head out every couple of weeks."

"And does Justin beat you up, too?"

"He certainly tries. Some days I hold my own better than others. Usually I just try to stick to the gym."

"Is there anyone who can take Justin down?"

"Marcus. He's the only one of us who has managed to get the best of him. He might not have the bulk of Justin, but he's quick and so good at reading people. It's like he can tell what Justin's going to do before he does it."

"Justin isn't just cutting him some slack because he's the boss?"

Eric shook his head. "There's a history between those two. Not sure what it is, but Justin has never taken it easy on Marcus or Alex."

"I never really thought much about the people you worked with, but it's been kind of fun getting to know Than and Justin."

Before he could reply, their mom came over. "Brooke and Lucas will be coming a little later so we can go ahead and eat."

The rest of the family joined them at the table and once grace was said for the meal, they began to dish up their food. Victoria found that the nerves she'd been fighting for the past day or so had diminished her appetite, but she ate just so her mom wouldn't get after her.

They were sitting around the table discussing the benefits of waiting for dessert or having it right away when Brooke, Lucas and Danny arrived. Brooke and Lucas had their arms around each other as they made their way from the gate to where the family sat. As soon as Victoria saw Danny's face, she knew they had news to share. The boy looked like he was going to burst with excitement.

"Can I tell them now, Mom?" he asked, his gaze going to Brooke. He was practically dancing.

Brooke grinned at him. After looking up at Lucas, she nodded. "Go ahead, sweetheart."

Danny swung around with a huge smile on his face. "Uncle Lucas asked Mom to marry him, and she said yes!"

Her mom got up so fast her chair tipped over backwards, but she ignored it as she moved toward the couple and wrapped her arms around Brooke. "Congratulations, sweetheart!"

Eric stood along with their dad to congratulate Lucas. "Welcome to the family, man. I hope you know what you're in for."

"Oh, I know." Lucas pressed a kiss to the top of Brooke's head. "Just one of the many reasons I knew I had to get her to marry me."

"Details!" Victoria demanded, delighted at the news and also glad to have something besides her surgery to talk about.

Brooke settled into the chair next to her, contentment and happiness evident on her face. "We went to Amber and Thom's restaurant since that was where we had our first 'date.' And he proposed to me over chocolate soufflé."

"Let me see your ring."

Brooke held out her hand. Given Lucas's wealth, Victoria had thought it would be a large diamond, but the dainty ring with a subtle diamond setting was just perfect for Brooke.

"It's beautiful. I'm so happy for you two."

"Have you set a date?" her mom asked.

Brooke glanced at Lucas then back to her mom. "It's going to be a few months. Maybe January."

"A winter wedding? Are you sure?"

"Well, it will be winter here, but not where we plan to have the wedding."

"You're not getting married here?" Victoria asked.

"No," Lucas said. "I have a friend who owns an island in the Caribbean, and we'll be flying everyone down there for the wedding."

Victoria did some quick calculations in her head and if things went the way they had for her previous surgery, she should be crutch-free by January. She really wanted to be able to enjoy the wedding and being at a beach.

This latest development just proved that her catching the bouquet at Staci and Eric's wedding hadn't been an indication of what the future held. Which was fine. Brooke deserved this happiness with Lucas.

Her thoughts went to Trent, and once again she wondered if her initial reluctance to get involved with him—combined with him seeing her on crutches—had caused that ship to sail. Sadness seeped into her heart, edging away some of the excitement and happiness. But she supposed it was better that she find this out before things had gotten serious. Chances were this wouldn't be the last surgery she had.

"Hey, Tori."

Victoria blinked, her gaze going to Brooke. "I'm sorry. What did you say?"

"I said that I'd like you to be my maid of honor."

"Are you sure?" The thoughts that had plagued her at the movie theater returned. She hoped the smile she gave Brooke hid the pain as she said, "You know you don't have to ask me to be in your wedding party just because we're sisters."

"Of course I'm sure. Why would you even ask that?" Brooke tilted her head and frowned. "Don't you want to be in my wedding party? You didn't have a problem being in Eric's."

She'd also felt closer to Staci than she had to Brooke, but Victoria figured now was not the time to point that out. Her gaze flicked to Eric, and she saw that he immediately understood what she was struggling with. Since his return three years earlier, he'd made the effort to spend time with her, and they were closer now than they'd ever been before.

She wished that was true of her relationship with Brooke, but it wasn't and might never be.

Victoria looked back at her sister and smiled. "I'd love to be in your wedding party. But you have to promise no puffy pageant-style dresses for me."

Brooke hesitated as if she didn't quite believe Victoria but then she said, "No worries. I think it's going to be pretty simple. You know I'm not really into that sort of thing."

The rest of the evening consisted of talk of the wedding, but Victoria had a hard time concentrating and finally gave up. After assuring everyone she was just tired, she said her goodbyes and headed for home. There were a ton of things she wanted to get done around the house the next day. Even though her mom was going to be there afterwards, Victoria didn't want her to have to do everything. Plus, it was a nice distraction from the worries plaguing her.

So even though it wasn't quite nine thirty when she got home, she quickly went through her night-time regimen and crawled into bed. She really wished that the next day had held time at the range, but it was likely to be several weeks before she could go shooting again—if ever. The thought of doing it without Trent sort of took away some of the pleasure she'd felt about practicing her new skill.

Trent walked into the office on Monday morning feeling more like himself than he had in a while. Getting a break from the reminders of Victoria and being away from the pitying looks Eric would likely have given him had helped somewhat. Yes, it still hurt to think that Victoria was involved with another guy, but above all else, he did want her to be happy. So if this other man could bring her more happiness than she would have found with him then he would accept that.

In the meantime, he just needed to keep his distance from the McKinleys until the hurt had eased enough that he didn't feel like his heart was bleeding all over the place at the mention of Victoria's name or the sight of her. He'd even gone to a different service than usual at church the day before to avoid running into Eric and Staci.

But it was Monday and over a week since his heart had been broken, so he knew it was time to face things head-on. As he walked to the open area between all their offices where the assistant he shared with Eric and Than sat, Trent noticed that Eric's office was dark. That was very unusual, and he hoped that nothing was wrong with Staci or Sarah.

Coming to a stop in front of his assistant's desk, he jerked his head towards Eric's office. "Where's Eric? He's usually in by now."

"He took a family day. One of his sisters is having surgery, I think."

Trent felt his stomach clench. "Do you know which one?"

She shook her head. "He didn't say who, just that he'd be out the whole day but could be contacted by phone or email."

"Okay. Thanks. Do you have stuff for me from last week?"

The woman nodded and handed him a folder. "Everything's in there. Most important is on top down to least important."

"Thanks, Mair."

Back in his office, Trent turned his phone over in his hand a few times. Text or phone. Finally he decided on a text. If Eric was available to talk, hopefully he would call.

Heard you're out for a family medical reason today. Hope everything is okay.

He set his phone down and flipped open the file Mair had given him. He'd barely had time to glance at the first paper when his phone rang.

Eric.

"Hey, Trent," Eric said when he answered.

"Everything okay? Mair said someone was having surgery?"

"Yeah, Victoria's having hip replacement surgery today." Eric hesitated then said, "Didn't she tell you?"

Trent felt like he'd just been kicked in the stomach. *Again*. He swallowed hard. "No. No, she didn't tell me. We haven't really talked for a couple of weeks."

There was a pause then Eric said, "Wait. I thought she talked to you last weekend. She said she'd called you to go shooting, but you weren't feeling well."

"I wasn't." Trent rubbed his forehead. "We didn't talk long."

"So you don't know anything that's been happening?"

"Just what you told me that night at your folks' place."

"Oh boy. I'm so sorry, man. For some reason, I got the impression that you guys had talked, and she'd told you about everything that had gone on. Although, now that I think about it, the fact that she didn't know where you were this week should have clued me in."

"What's going on, Eric? I feel like I've missed a bunch of important stuff."

"Yeah, you have, but first, I need to set the record straight. She wasn't out on a date with Dan that Friday night."

"She wasn't?" Trent was flooded by such a wave of conflicting emotions he didn't know what he felt at Eric's revelation.

"No. Dan had offered to buy her portion of the company she and Dad started. They were out discussing details about it that night and then when they came to the house, they met with Dad to bring him up to speed."

"She sold her part of the company?"

"Yeah, apparently she'd been thinking about it for a while, and his offer was just what she needed. She planned to use the money to fund her hip surgery, but then Lucas stepped up and offered to pay for it so she could save that money for her future."

"Lucas paid for her surgery?" *He* could have helped her with that if only he'd known that the reason she'd been waiting had been financial. But no, he'd acted like a stupid fool and assumed the worst about everything.

"Yeah. Totally out of the blue, but a real blessing for her since her deductible was so high on her insurance. I didn't realize until this came to light that that's why she's waited so long to have the surgery on this hip. She had the other one done about three years ago but kept putting off having this one done. She's stubborn, that sister of mine. Determined to prove to the world that she can do it all by herself."

Trent closed his eyes and bent his head forward. "What time is her surgery?"

"She's supposed to go in around ten. They said that if all goes well, she should be in recovery a couple hours later. If you want to see her, why don't you come up after work? She should be in her own room by then and up for visitors."

The question was, would she want to see him? He wouldn't blame her if she didn't. But he'd go up and test the waters. If she didn't throw him out, he'd take that as a sign that perhaps he would be able to repair the damage he'd done over the past couple of weeks with his inability to communicate with her how he felt.

"I'll drop by. I'd come sooner, but I've got a whack of stuff to catch up on. Marcus wouldn't be happy if I ducked out too early."

"No worries. She's going to be out of it for a good chunk of the day anyway."

After ending the call with Eric, Trent sat for a moment trying to wrap his head around everything. He had no idea what to expect from Victoria, but he intended to stick by her side until she told him to his face to get out of her life. If that was what she truly wanted, he would respect that, but if he had a chance to fix the mess he'd made of everything, he was going to take it.

CHAPTER FOURTEEN

IT **WAS** midafternoon before Victoria felt like the fog had finally cleared from her head. She'd woken shivering and disoriented in the recovery room. Though she had some pain, they were keeping her well medicated. Everything she went through the first time around came rushing back. She assumed it was somewhat like childbirth where a woman forgot the pain but that the memory of it came back once labor started with a subsequent pregnancy.

It was all coming back with shocking clarity and for a few minutes in the recovery room—okay, maybe for more than just a *few* minutes—she'd regretted putting herself through it again. She had just kept repeating *no more crutches* as she lay in the bed trying to push the pain from her mind.

Now the pain was finally under control with the help of some medication. Her mom was hovering over her, and she'd had a steady stream of family in and out of her room. She'd dozed off and on throughout the rest of the afternoon.

Victoria had been lying there with her eyes closed, wishing her mother would stop asking her how she was feeling, when she heard a familiar voice.

Trent?

She tried to keep her breathing even, suddenly not sure she wanted to face him. It was almost a given that she looked awful. No makeup. Hair matted around her head. Yeah, not exactly how she'd wanted to look when she saw him again. Particularly since she wasn't at all sure how things stood between them.

"Tori, darling. Are you awake?"

Her mother's voice was soft, but Victoria knew there was no way she could fake sleep now. Her heart pounded in her chest, and her eyelids were desperately trying to lift of their own accord. Letting out a quick breath, she opened her eyes and found her mom at her bedside.

"I'm awake. Just resting."

"Trent's here, and he's brought some absolutely gorgeous flowers for you."

Her mom stepped back and motioned with her hand. Trent stepped into view, a large colorful bouquet of flowers in his hands. She drank in the sight of him. He was still wearing his suit which meant he must have come straight from the office. The smile he gave her as he moved closer to the bed was more tentative than she would have expected from him. But he was still so handsome, and he was there. For her.

"I'll just go find something to put those in," her mom said as she took the flowers from Trent and left the room.

In that moment, part of her wished that Lucas hadn't arranged for a private room for her. The silence was heavy between them.

Trent snagged a chair and pulled it closer to the bed. After he had settled on it, he looked at her, his blue eyes serious. "How are you feeling?"

"Better since they gave me drugs. I had some pain coming out of surgery, but it's pretty much gone now."

He stared at her without saying anything for what seemed like an eternity, then his gaze dropped from hers briefly. "I'm sorry."

Of all the things she'd thought he'd say none of them had been an apology. "Sorry? For what?"

He paused for a moment, almost as if trying to figure out the answer to her question. "For not keeping in contact better. I let some...things distract me, and I'm sorry. I was shocked to hear that you were having your surgery today."

"There was nothing you could have done, even if you'd known," Victoria said. Though she would have loved to have had him there before the surgery to distract her and keep her from focusing on it too much.

Trent leaned forward, bracing his elbows on his thighs, his hands clasped between his knees. "At the very least, I could have been praying for you as you prepared for the surgery. Or offered to help with anything you needed to do ahead of time." He hesitated. "And I could have done what Lucas did for you."

Victoria frowned. "No. That wasn't supposed to be how this worked out."

"What? Why would you say that? You *knew* I had the financial means with which to help you with something like this. I didn't realize the reason you were waiting on the surgery on your hip was because you couldn't afford it. If I'd known, I would have offered to help you out."

"I know. But I have been praying for months for this to work out. When I got the offer on the business, I assumed that was God's way of answering my prayer. It wasn't until after that that Lucas offered his help. If it had been God's will for you to provide for my surgery, things would have turned out differently. But I'm actually glad it didn't work out that way."

Trent's brows drew together as he frowned. "Why?"

"I wouldn't have wanted that to have been part of our friendship. I would have felt like I owed you something I could never repay, but I would have still felt obliged to try."

Trent straightened, crossing his arms over his chest. "And you don't feel that way about Lucas?"

"No, I don't. He's already practically family, but more than that, he has a part of his company that deals with situations like mine. He didn't run mine through that division because it would likely be seen as a conflict of interest since he's so close to our family, but just knowing that this is something he's done for others made it easier for me to accept."

"You never even mentioned that you were considering surgery this seriously. You talked about it briefly that first day I saw you on crutches but then never after that," Trent said.

"I've been able to put it off for a few years, but in the last few months it seemed to get significantly worse which is why I ended up back on crutches all the time. Up until that point, I just tried to give my hip a break by using the crutches when I was by myself. I didn't want my folks to know how bad it had gotten. But when it got to where I had to decide between letting them know or falling and possibly doing more damage, I had to tuck my pride into my back pocket and resort to the crutches."

"Were you in much pain?"

She saw the concern and care in Trent's gaze and felt her heart clench. Now was not the time to think about how she felt about him. It would be too easy to misread his actions and concerned words when she was feeling vulnerable on so many levels.

"I was, but not anymore. Of course, right now it's the drugs that are helping with that, but I remember from last time that once the pain from the incision goes away, there should be no pain from the hip itself."

"Hey, Victoria," Eric said as he walked into the room. He smiled when he saw Trent. "Glad you were able to make it up."

He settled into another chair, and the three of them chatted until her mom returned. Eric and Trent left briefly to go get something to eat. In that time, her dad and Brooke showed up and, a short time later, so did Alicia. Brooke didn't stay too long since she had to pick Danny up from Lucas's mom's house. Alicia stayed a while longer but then she left as well. Trent and Eric and her parents stayed until visiting hours were over before saying goodnight and leaving her on her own. Her mother had been reluctant to go, but the nurses had assured her they'd take good care of her baby girl.

Once everyone had gone, Victoria settled down with her tablet to read a little before trying to sleep. She hadn't gotten very far before the nurses came in to check her bandages and make sure her pain was still under control.

She'd just started to read again when her phone chirped. Frowning, she reached for it and saw she had a text from Trent.

CHAPTER FIFTEEN

WHAT *happens to a frog's car when it breaks down?*

Victoria stared at it for a moment then replied. *I don't know. What?*

It gets toad.

It was so dumb she couldn't help the chuckle that escaped. *Haha*

What did the duck say when she bought lipstick?

I don't know.

Put it on my bill.

Oh my goodness. Where are you getting these? Badjokesareus.com? LOL

You don't like my jokes?

Wellll....

Last one: What nails do carpenters hate to hit?

Hah. I know this one. Fingernails.

Smartie. ☺ Well, I'll let you sleep now...just wanted to make you smile.

You succeeded! Thank you. Have a good night.

You, too, babe. Goodnight.

Victoria lowered her phone and leaned back against her pillows, a smile on her face. Yes, he had succeeded in making her smile and lifting her spirits. But most of all, he'd taken another little piece of her heart. Not many more and he'd have it all...but did it matter to him?

Trent wanted to take another gift up to the hospital but didn't want to bring more flowers. He stopped at Walmart on his way and after looking around for a bit, he picked up a stuffed bear, a big candy bar and a couple of puzzle books. He didn't know how long she was going to be in the hospital but figured he'd bring her something to keep her busy if it were more than a day or two.

He poked his head in and saw that it was just Mrs. McKinley and Victoria there. Victoria looked like she was asleep, but her mom looked up from the book in her hand as he stepped into the room. A smile spread across her face.

"Hi, Trent. C'mon in." She waved him over.

Victoria turned her head and opened her eyes as he walked to where her mom sat. She smiled at him, but he could see there was strain on her face.

"I'm going to go get something to drink," her mom said as she stood up. "You can have my seat, Trent."

After she had left, he turned toward the bed and held out the stuffed bear. "Thought you might like some company."

Another quick smile crossed her face as she took the bear and ran her fingers over its fur. "Thank you, Trent. He's cute."

"Um, the bow around the neck is pink...pretty sure that makes it a she."

This time the smile she gave him lingered a bit longer. "Men secure in their masculinity wear pink. It's a he."

Returning her smile, he pulled the chair her mom had vacated closer to the bed and sat down. "I also brought you some chocolate and puzzle books in case you get bored."

He reached out to set them on the small table that was in place over her bed. She immediately picked up the chocolate bar and ran a finger under the wrapper to open it.

"How did you know this was my favorite?" she asked as she broke off a piece of the chocolate and put it into her mouth.

"I saw one sitting on your counter while I was there one day. And I figured if you didn't like it, I'd eat it since it happens to be a favorite of mine, too. Of course, I'll eat pretty much anything that involves chocolate and nuts."

She broke off another piece and held it out to him. "Thank you. It was just what I needed."

"Bad day?" Trent asked. He popped the square into his mouth and let it melt a bit before chewing it.

"Just a little. I turned wrong at some point and something happened with the incision, so they had to check it to make sure I hadn't torn a stitch out. It was bleeding, but thankfully nothing had torn, although they did have to re-bandage it. So I was in a bit more pain today." She looked away from him and took a quick breath and let it out.

When her eyelashes fluttered, Trent realized she was holding back tears. He scooted the chair forward so he could take her hand. It felt so small and fragile in his even though he knew it was anything but. "Hey now. You know you don't need to be strong all the time."

Her head dipped forward, and a large tear ran down her cheek and dropped onto the sheet covering her hips and legs. She took a couple of deep breaths, and her grip on his hand tightened, but she still didn't look at him. "It's just been hard with Mom here, too. I couldn't be completely honest about the pain levels because I didn't want her to worry."

"I understand. But I'm here and I can handle it, so if you need a shoulder to cry on..."

She looked at him, her eyes like melted chocolate. "Thank you."

He wished he could just scoop her up and hold her close so she could have a good cry, but physical limitations aside, that wasn't his place. Yet. "Has the pain lessened now?"

"Pretty much. Mom went to the bathroom while the nurse was here, and I was able to tell her I needed more. That was about forty-five minutes ago, so it's finally taking effect." Her shoulders slumped a little. "I was supposed to get out of bed for a bit today, but after that happened they want me to wait so I don't aggravate things further."

"Just take it slow, babe. In a month, this will all be behind you. You'll look back and realize this was just a blip on the road to recovery, not a significant setback."

She took another deep breath and blew it out. "Sorry. Didn't mean to fall apart on you."

"Hey, that's what friends are for. What me to tell you some more jokes?"

That got a smile from her, and the moisture in her eyes disappeared. "You can save those for later." She gave his hand a squeeze and then loosened her grip.

He took that as a sign and let his hand slip from hers. Leaning back in the chair, Trent stretched his legs out under the edge of her bed. "I've got a million of them."

She rolled her eyes at him. "Have you and Danny been having conversations? That kid has a million of them, too."

Trent winked at her, happy to see the strain had eased from her face. "I never reveal my sources."

"You boys always stick together," Victoria said as she reached for another piece of chocolate. "So, tell me how your day went. It had to be better than mine."

"Only in that I'm not in a hospital bed." Trent let out a sigh. "Had to update Marcus on the information we've gathered after the hacking attempt. I should have done it last week but had to go on that trip with Than instead. Anyway, it wasn't the news I had hoped to be able to give him. Even with all the coding we had to analyze and the fact that Tracer got close to finding his location, we still have no idea who it was or why they targeted BlackThorpe."

Before she could respond, there was noise at the door, and Trent looked over to see Eric come into the room with his family and his mom.

"Auntie Tori!" Sarah dashed over to the far side of the bed and rested her arms and chin on the edge of it. "Are you feeling better?"

Victoria reached out and stroked the blonde hair of her niece. "Now that you're here, I'm feeling perfect. How are you doing?"

Trent grinned as he listened to the little girl recount pretty much every move she'd made that day. He looked up at Eric, not surprised to see him regarding his daughter with unabashed adoration. Staci, on the other hand, just smiled and shook her head. Something told Trent that she heard a lot more of Sarah's ramblings than Eric did.

She moved closer to her husband, and Eric reached out to pull her against his side. Though they weren't over the top with kissing or anything like that, they were one of the most affectionate couples Trent had ever been around. It was rare when they were in the same room that they weren't connected in some away, whether it was holding hands, hugging or having their arms around each other. He was glad that his friend had found such happiness after the pain of discovering that he'd missed the first five years of his daughter's life.

"Do you need anything?" Caroline McKinley said when Sarah finally finished her account of her day. "More pain pills? Some water?"

"I'm fine, Mom."

Trent stood up and motioned for Caroline to take his chair. There were others in the room, but this one was closest to her daughter. He went to stand next to Eric and Staci.

"Didn't expect to see you here again," Eric said, his gaze steady on him.

Trent shrugged. "I didn't have anything else to do. Figured I'd come see how she was doing."

"I'm sure she appreciated that," Eric said as he looked to where Victoria sat.

They were interrupted by someone bringing Victoria's dinner. Her dad arrived around the same time so Trent went with Eric, Staci and Sarah to the cafeteria. When they returned an hour later, Caroline and Doug went down to get something to eat.

While they were chatting, Brooke and Lucas showed up, hand in hand.

"How are you feeling, Victoria?" Lucas asked as they approached her bedside. "You're looking great."

Victoria smiled. "I'm doing better. Thank you."

"Are they treating you well?" Brooke asked, concern in her eyes.

"Yep. Can't complain at all about the staff. They've been nothing but helpful. I do wish Mom wouldn't hover quite so much, but I remember that from the last time, too. I'm not sure if I'm going to be able to handle that much hovering for the next few weeks."

Brooke laughed. "Better you than me, sweetheart. That would definitely send me round the bend."

"Is that your way of saying you wouldn't want me to hover over you if you were feeling sick? Even though our vows will say in sickness and in health?" Lucas asked with a grin.

Brooke reached up to cup his cheek. "Oh, no. You can hover all you want. In fact, I insist on you hovering over me. Every single day for the rest of our lives."

It was then that Trent spotted the ring on Brooke's hand as she lowered it to her side. "Hey! Are congratulations in order?"

Brooke looked at him and raised her hand again. "Oh, you mean this?"

"Uh. Yeah. That."

"They got engaged Friday night," Victoria told him.

"Well, congratulations, you two." Trent went around the bed to shake Lucas's hand and give Brooke a hug. "Guess you didn't need to catch the bouquet or garter after all, eh?"

As the group laughed, Trent wondered if there would come a point that he'd be able to make a similar announcement with Victoria. He just kept telling himself to be patient. She had a lot on her plate at the moment. And while he wasn't going to push her for anything just yet, it was hard to wait. He'd thought he'd already lost her once and didn't want to risk that again.

For now he'd focus on their friendship. He was going to be the best friend she'd ever had. Friendship was always a good basis for a relationship, and they were going to have a great friendship on which to build. That was his goal anyway.

Not wanting to intrude on their family time, Trent edged close to the bed and touched her hand. "I'm going to go. Have a good night. And if you need some jokes, just text me."

She looked up at him, her eyes wide. "I will. Thank you. For everything."

"Anytime, babe." He straightened and said goodbye to the rest of the family before leaving the room. He knew they were curious about what was going on between him and Victoria, but he wasn't going to be giving up any details until he was more sure of that himself.

Victoria found herself watching the clock the next afternoon. She knew that Trent usually worked until five, and the two nights he'd come to the hospital, he'd been there by five thirty. Though she was still stuck in the bed for the most part, her mom had helped her with her hair, and she'd put on a bit of makeup. After two days of looking blah, it had been a definite mood booster to feel like she looked more like her normal self.

Her mom had had a dinner date with her dad and some friends, so Victoria was alone when Trent showed up, once again bearing gifts.

She lifted her eyebrows when he handed her another bear. It was similar to the one he'd brought the previous day except the fur was a different color and the ribbon was blue.

"I thought Mr. Bear could use some company from Miss Bear," he said as she took it.

She gave the bear a squeeze and stroked its fur. "So no choice this time, huh? Definitely female?"

"Definitely female," Trent said as he set another chocolate bar on the table. He also put down a bottle of her favorite drink. "Thought you might be missing this, too."

Her heart clenched at how he thoughtful he was to remember the things she liked. "I have been missing it."

Trent picked the bottle back up and twisted off the lid before handing it to her. "Enjoy."

He settled into the chair as he had the day before. "No one here today?"

"Mom was here earlier, but she and Dad had dinner plans with friends who were just passing through on their way to Chicago." She shifted a little. "They got me out of bed for a bit."

Trent looked pleasantly surprised at the news. "Really? How did that go?"

"Well, I won't be running races any time soon, and I'm still on crutches, but it went pretty good. It's a start."

And being able to move around had meant the removal of a few other things that had been necessary but somewhat uncomfortable. They wanted to make sure all parts of her body were working correctly before even discussing a going-home plan. She really hoped they'd let her leave the hospital by the weekend. Being in her own home would be a wonderful thing.

It ended up being Saturday before Victoria was finally discharged from the hospital. She had been going crazy even though she knew it was the best place to be until the doctor cleared her to leave. They sent her home with a wheelchair as well, though she was determined to use it as little as possible.

But she was thankful that her house was all one level in case she did need it.

Her mom had been at the house during the day on Saturday to prepare dinner for the family except for Brooke, Lucas and Danny who had other plans. Trent was there once again, and no one seemed surprised to see him around anymore. He had stopped showing up with a gift each time, although he still did bring chocolate when he noticed she was out.

Sleeping in her own bed that night was heaven. It was so much more restful without having the nurses coming in and out to check on her. Each day she'd gotten better at maneuvering on her crutches while still being careful to not aggravate the incision. It would still be a little bit longer before she was as confident on the crutches as she'd been before the surgery.

Not really wanting to have a bunch of people asking her questions if she showed up at church in a wheelchair, Victoria opted to stay home on Sunday morning. Alicia had volunteered to come over and hang with her parents went to church.

"These are beyond yummy, Alicia." Victoria pulled a chunk off the moist, gooey cinnamon bun and popped it into her mouth. "Where did you get them?"

Alicia sat on the other end of the couch, her feet tucked up under her. She also had a cinnamon bun in her hand. "They're from a bakery not far from the office. The girls at work took me there one day. I try to only stop by once every couple of weeks."

Victoria grinned. "I can see why. They're divine."

"So, what's up with Trent?" Alicia asked. She set her cinnamon bun back down on the plate in her lap and licked her fingers.

"Have no idea," Victoria said as she shifted on the couch.

"He's been at the hospital every day and you have no idea? I'd say—given previous interactions with him—that he's trying to show you that he's interested in you."

Victoria shrugged. "He's been blowing a bit hot and cold over the past few weeks. I'm not going to assume anything at this point."

Alicia sighed. "You guys have been dancing around each other for ages now. Someone has to make a move. If he did tell you he wanted something more serious than just friendship, what would you say?"

What would she say? Good question. "Part of me would want to agree."

"But the other part?"

"Well, that part would be afraid that things would end just like they have any other time I've tried to date a guy of average height. And it would be much more awkward since he's Eric's friend."

"I think you'd better make up your mind because I have a feeling that conversation with Trent is going to happen sooner rather than later."

Victoria looked at Alicia and frowned. "You do? Did he say something to you?"

"Nope, but it's pretty obvious he has it bad for you. And this is way more than the lighthearted attempts he's made to get you to go out with him in the past. You might not see it, but everyone else can see how he looks at you. How he tries to make you smile."

He did make her smile, that was for sure. But would that be enough? She'd been praying about it but didn't really feel peace either way. She thought back to the conversation she'd had with her group of little people friends. Most of their responses with regards to being with an average-size man had to do with the physical side of the relationship, and while that was something Victoria had considered, it wasn't the main thing.

Some of the group had experiences similar to hers. Others had worse—they'd actually ended up in relationships with people who did view their stature as a fetish thing. Thankfully, that wasn't something Victoria had ever thought about with Trent. There had been one woman in the group who was married to an average-size man, but she was a very vocal person who would get in the face of anyone who dared look at her wrong. She obviously didn't let the way some in society viewed her marriage to her average-size husband bother her.

Which was where Victoria knew she needed to end up if she could even hope to have a future with Trent.

"Have you ever had a serious relationship?" Victoria asked.

Alicia hesitated then said, "Well, not super serious, but it lasted almost nine months."

"Why did you break up?"

"It just kind of fizzled out around the time of my mom's accident and then my decision to move here." Alicia took a bite of her cinnamon roll. "Like I said, it wasn't super serious."

"Would you say yes to Trent if you were in my shoes?"

Alicia regarded her intently. "If all I had to go on was Trent's character, I would say yes. And it doesn't hurt that he's easy on the eyes." A quick smile curved Alicia's lips. "Seriously though, I know there are more things to consider for you."

Victoria nodded. "Trent needs to understand that being with someone like me won't be easy."

"I think that an honest conversation with Trent is in order if he broaches the subject of something more serious. Just put it all out there. Maybe it will make him back off and if so, at least you weren't too involved. But if he doesn't back off, he knows what he's getting into."

Victoria stared down at the half-eaten cinnamon roll on her plate. Rejection sooner rather than later? It was a risk she needed to decide if she wanted to take.

CHAPTER SIXTEEN

TRENT didn't make it over to Victoria's on Sunday like he had hoped. But after work on Monday, he dropped by his apartment to change into a pair of shorts and a T-shirt and grab a bite to eat before heading over to her place. There was only her car parked in the driveway, but he knew her mom was there with her.

"Hello, Trent," Caroline said when she opened the door. "C'mon in."

Trent stepped into the coolness of the house. "Hope it's okay I stopped by." It felt a bit different from when he went to see her at the hospital.

"It's fine. In fact, I might impose on you to take her out for a little while."

"Take her out?" Trent asked as they walked toward the kitchen. He didn't see any sign of Victoria.

"I think she's feeling a little housebound. Maybe you could convince her to go out for ice cream or to the park. Get her a little fresh air."

"Sure. I can do that." He glanced around. "Where is she?"

"She's lying down. The physical therapist came by today to work with her. I think it kind of wore her out a little."

Trent wasn't happy to hear that. She'd just been through major surgery. Surely they could give her a bit of a break.

"I'll go see how she is. Make yourself at home," Caroline said as she walked toward the hallway that led to the bedrooms.

He went to the kitchen and opened the fridge to see if there was something to drink. Spotting his favorite soda on the shelf filled him with warmth. As far as he knew, it wasn't something she drank, so its presence there meant she'd bought it for him. He grabbed one and twisted the lid off.

He'd just taken a deep swallow when he heard voices and turned to see Victoria and Caroline headed his way. As they got closer, he could see the strain on her face just like that day in the hospital.

But she still smiled when she saw him. "Hi, Trent."

"Heya, babe. How about we go out for a bit?"

"Out? Where?" Victoria leaned forward on her crutches, shifting her weight.

"We can go through a drive-thru to get some ice cream and maybe go to the park."

She hesitated, but he could see that she was considering it. Looking up at her mom, she said, "You'll be okay on your own here, Mom?"

"I'll be fine, darling. Actually, your dad is on his way over so I won't be alone."

"If we're going to go any distance, we'd better bring the wheelchair," Victoria said.

Since she'd just had a workout on her hip, Trent had hoped she'd suggest it. If she hadn't, he would have. "I think that's a great idea. Where is it?"

"In the hallway."

Trent saw the relieved expression on Caroline's face as he headed for the hall. He hoped that it wasn't something more than just the physical therapy that had caused Caroline's concern for her daughter. He pushed the wheelchair into the living room.

"Do you want me to push you out to the car or can you walk?" he asked Victoria.

She had taken a seat at the dining room table, her crutches still on her arms. "I think I can walk. It's not too far."

"Well, let me take this out. Take your time."

He left the front door open after he'd pushed the wheelchair out. It didn't take him long to get it folded and into the back of his car. When he came around to the passenger side, he saw Victoria coming toward him, Caroline a few feet behind her. He was about to ask about getting the stool for her when he realized that it probably wasn't going to do her much good.

Caroline stood at the front of his car watching them as Victoria neared him.

"Is it okay if I just lift you onto the seat, babe? I'm not sure you want to try the stool just yet, do you?"

She looked at him for a moment before her gaze slid away, and she nodded. "Yeah, I probably can't maneuver from the stool onto the seat just yet."

"Well then, be prepared to be swept off your feet." Trent tried to keep his tone light even though his pulse had kicked up a notch at the thought of holding Victoria in his arms. He positioned himself so when he picked her up, she would be facing the right way to just slide onto the seat. The last thing he wanted was to do anything that might hurt her. "Ready?"

Her hesitation was brief, but he still saw it before she nodded. Bending down, he slid one arm around her back and the other under her knees. She kept the crutches in her grip as he lifted her up and put her on the seat. It had been a brief moment of contact, but the scent of her still lingered, teasing his senses.

"Let me take those," Trent said as she slid her arms free of the cuffs on the crutches. He put them on the back seat and then went around to the driver's side and slid behind the wheel. He looked over at her as he started up the car. "Everything okay? Does the seatbelt hurt your incision?"

She shook her head but didn't meet his gaze. "It's fine."

Trent found a nearby Dairy Queen and got them both Blizzards. He then checked his phone for the nearest park. "Have you been there before?"

"Yes. It's a nice one," Victoria said.

It only took about ten minutes to get there, but it seemed like an eternity because Victoria remained silent for most of it. Thankfully, the park seemed fairly empty when they arrived. He parked the car and then got the wheelchair out. After positioning it and making sure the wheels were locked, he opened Victoria's door. She already had her seatbelt off and was clutching her ice cream in her hands.

"Ready?"

At her nod, he once again picked her up and gently set her in the wheelchair. Her head was bent, but he heard her say, "Thank you."

His gut clenched as he looked at her sitting there, so fragile-looking. He dropped to his heels so they were eye to eye. "What's wrong, babe?"

She let out a sigh and gestured to the wheelchair. "I just feel like it's such a pain for you to have to cart this around and lift me in and out. I'm sorry."

Trent chuckled. "Don't be sorry. Holding you in my arms is no hardship at all." He gave her a quick wink and watched as her cheeks turned pink and a small smile tugged at the corners of her mouth. "Let's go find a place to eat this ice cream. You'll need to hold mine so I can drive this thing."

He reached into the car and grabbed his Blizzard to give to Victoria. After locking up the car, Trent freed the wheels on the chair and guided it down a paved path that led toward a small pond. He found a shaded bench that faced the water and pushed the wheelchair to a stop in front of it. After checking to make sure the wheels were secure once again, he settled onto the bench next to her.

"Is this okay?" A breeze brushed across his skin and caused the leaves in the tree above them to rustle.

Victoria's eyes closed, and she lifted her face. When she opened her eyes, she smiled at him. "Yes. It's perfect." She took a deep breath. "I needed to get out."

"Yeah, your mom said she thought you did." He took the ice cream she held out to him.

While they ate their ice cream, Trent talked about his day, hoping she'd open up about hers as well. When she asked him questions about what he shared, Trent realized that she seemed genuinely interested in what he did.

At one point, she asked how Than and Justin were doing.

"Justin's wondering when we're coming back out to the range. And Than...well, he's still Than."

"I won't be shooting for a little while," Victoria said, a rueful smile on her face.

"When do you think you'll be back to full strength?" Trent asked. He had missed their times at the range, even more so knowing that he could have had more time with her there if he hadn't been such an idiot.

"Since it's my left hip, I can probably start driving again in a couple of weeks. I would imagine I'd be able to shoot around the same time."

"Considering the pain you must have been in to stand and shoot, you did an excellent job."

Victoria smiled. "I'll be even better when I'm off my crutches altogether, and I can stand without any pain."

"You're going to be off your crutches completely?"

"Yep. The doctor said that about three months after my surgery I should be crutch-free."

Trent smiled. "That's terrific!"

"Yep. I won't have to go back on them until my hips start to go bad again."

"Go bad again?" Trent didn't like the sound of that.

"Yes. I'm so young having these hip replacements that they're going to need to be replaced at some point. I'm not talking about in the next few years, but it will have to be done again."

Trent hated to think of her having to go through it all again. He wished he could do something to spare her the pain, but he knew it was part of her life. She was strong though, and that was one of the things he loved about her.

Love.

The word flashed through his mind, startling him in its clarity. He'd tried very hard not to think about the L-word where Victoria was concerned. Oh, he knew how he felt, but he'd tried not to label it as love just yet, because it would be that much harder to get over if she rejected him.

He looked at her, his heart clenching at the serenity he saw on her face as she stared out across the water. Another gust of wind ruffled her hair, and he could already see that the strain had eased from her face once again.

And he knew it was time. He'd waited so long already. He just needed to know.

"Hey, Victoria," he said as he set his empty ice cream container on the bench next to him.

She turned to look at him, her expression expectant as her mouth curved into a smile. "Hey, Trent."

He wanted to stare at her forever, and yet he wanted to look away in case she could read his feelings for her all over his face. Instead, he cleared his throat and said, "Here's the thing. I know I made it apparent in the last several months or so that I like you."

Her eyes widened as the smile slowly faded from her face. That was not good. But Trent was determined.

"When you called me about your computer, I was surprised, but pleased. Until I realized just how bad off your system was. It was then I realized that my attitude toward you over the previous several months had made you not want to be around me. The exact opposite effect of what I wanted. So I decided that I wasn't going to be that pesky, annoying guy anymore. I wanted to show you that I could be a good friend, and then maybe you'd be willing to consider something more with me."

He paused to see if she'd say anything, but she just sat there, ice cream container clenched in her hands, staring at him. Not quite the response he was aiming for, but he pressed on.

"I enjoy spending time with you. Going to the shooting range. Having dinner together. I thought we were getting along really well."

This time she did nod, her expression relaxing a bit. Not enough, but it was better than nothing.

"But then that Friday night I was at your folks' place for the barbecue, Eric told me you were on a date." Trent glanced down at his hands briefly, the memory of how that news had hurt still rather fresh. "That was hard to take. And then I saw him with you and that was even worse."

"But I wasn't on a date with Dan," Victoria said, a frown tightening her features. "It was all business. He has a girlfriend in Chicago."

"Yes, I know that now, but apparently your mom had told Eric you were on a date. When you called me the next day..."

Her eyes widened. "You still thought..."

Feeling a bit chagrined, Trent gave a shake of his head. "I was an idiot. I'm sorry. It just...well, it just hurt." He swallowed past the tightness in his throat. "I guess what I want to say is this. I really like you, Victoria. And I want to know if you might feel the same way and be willing to give us a shot."

She caught her lip between her teeth but kept her dark gaze on his. "Alicia told me yesterday that this moment was coming. I've spent a lot of time since then thinking and praying about it. There's a lot to consider, Trent."

Trent nodded. "I'm not oblivious to the challenges that would lie ahead."

"It's more than just you being taller than me and the logistics challenge that might present. I know you're not talking marriage, but I can't date someone without knowing from the start that he can handle what my life might hold in the long run. I *have* to look that far down the road and make sure you know about the difficulties."

"Like what?"

"Well, like the additional surgeries I may face someday."

Trent frowned. "You think that would scare me off? The only reason I hate the thought of more surgeries is because of how it means you'll be in pain again."

Her gaze lowered and then lifted to meet his again. "Any child I have has a chance of inheriting my dwarfism."

"If I don't have a problem with that in you, I certainly wouldn't have a problem with it in a child."

"Even if it's a son?"

Trent paused for a second as he took in what she meant. "Babe, if anyone understands not meeting a father's expectation that would be me. I would never do that to any son of mine. I would have the same expectations of a child with dwarfism as I would an average-size child."

Victoria tilted her head, her brows drawn together. "You do realize that even though it's a good thing to challenge a child to do their best, there will be some things a child with dwarfism can't excel at?"

"Oh, I know. The expectations I would have for my children are that they be kind, gentle, and loving and that they are strong like you are." When she didn't say anything to that, Trent said, "I've thought about all this stuff. I learned what I could about your type of dwarfism and what it meant for you. I knew you likely wouldn't even consider anything with me if I didn't know what it entailed. So I tried to educate myself. But what it comes down to for me is that you're still the kindest, most loving, courageous, beautiful woman I've ever met. And I want to at least see where things might go between us. If that's what you want."

Victoria stared at him so long—her brown eyes dark with emotion—that he was afraid of what was going on in her head. Finally, she said, "Yes, I want that too."

Apprehension that he hadn't even been totally aware of suddenly left his body, and joy and love flooded in to replace it. Oh, he wouldn't share that with her yet, but it was still there waiting for the right moment. For now, he was just grateful that she was going to at least give them a shot. He would do everything in his power to convince her that it was the right thing. Because in his heart, he knew it was. He truly believed that God had placed this love in his heart for her and only her.

"We don't need to rush into dates or stuff like that because right now your healing is the most important thing. But we can do stuff like this, which I suppose could be considered a date." Trent paused, feeling a bit like he was bumbling his words. He couldn't believe she'd actually agreed. "And I want to be able to tell your brother we're dating as well as those guys at work when they ask me what's going on with you and me. Is that okay with you?"

A smile spread across her face and her eyes sparkled as she nodded. "That's just fine."

"You ready to go home?" Trent asked.

Victoria shook her head. No, she didn't want to go home. This was where she wanted to be. Sitting together as the breeze cooled the warm day. Watching the day shift from afternoon to evening and listening to the ducks on the pond. "Not unless there's some place *you* have to go."

His gaze warmed her as he said, "I'm exactly where I want to be."

They stayed at the park for the next hour. After Trent had gotten up to throw away their ice cream cups, he'd settled back onto the bench, and they'd just talked. He told her more about his family, including the fact that his sister had been in town a couple of weekends earlier. Since he knew pretty much everything about *her* family, Victoria shared a bit of what it was like growing up as a little person.

Looking out across the pond, Victoria saw that the sky was beginning to darken as the breeze picked up a little force. "Was there rain in the forecast?"

"No clue," Trent said. "But it kinda looks like there might be. Guess we'd better head back to the house."

Though it wasn't what Victoria wanted, she knew getting caught in the rain wouldn't be the best thing for her. One day she could dance in the rain, but it wouldn't be quite yet.

Trent pushed the wheelchair back along the path to where he'd parked the car. This time when he picked her up to put her into the car, he didn't release her quite as quickly. He grabbed the seatbelt and leaned across her to slip it into the buckle. She inhaled the subtle scent of him, noticing that this close up, the bit of stubble on his cheeks was more apparent.

He glanced at her as he moved back, and she could see the flecks of dark blue in his eyes. His gaze dropped briefly to her mouth, but he straightened and gave her a smile. She saw a raindrop land on his shirt, darkening the fabric.

Trent looked up at the sky. "Guess we timed that right."

By the time he was behind the wheel, the raindrops were splattering more frequently on the windshield. Over the course of the drive to her house, the rain came down in a torrent. Trent turned up the speed of the wipers to keep the windshield clear as he guided the car through the traffic.

When he pulled to a stop in her driveway, he stared out the front window and then glanced over at her. "Well, we could make a run for it or sit and see if the rain eases up a bit."

Since she was in no condition to run anywhere, Victoria said, "Let's wait it out."

He shut the car off then reached over and took her hand in his, intertwining their fingers. Victoria looked down at their hands. Hers looked so small in his larger, stronger one. But sitting there in the car, side by side, their difference in height didn't seem as apparent. His thumb stroked across the back of her hand, but he didn't say anything, just let the sound of the rain beating down on the car fill the silence between them.

Victoria closed her eyes and rested her head back against the seat. She wanted to seal every moment of this afternoon with Trent in her memory, in her heart. It had been so perfectly them. Part of her was almost afraid that she'd fallen asleep after her PT session and that it had all been a dream.

"Hey. What's wrong?" Trent's voice interrupted her thoughts. When she opened her eyes and turned to look at him, he said, "You've got a small hand, but that grip just about broke my fingers."

Immediately, she relaxed her hold on him. She'd been totally unaware that she'd been squeezing his hand so tightly. "Sorry about that."

"Hey, I can take it." He tilted his head as his gaze remained on her. "But it does make me curious what was going through your head to cause such a reaction."

Victoria stared at him, wondering if she should tell him. His eyes were soft with an expectation she couldn't deny. "I was just wondering if maybe this was a dream. That I'd wake up and be in my bed."

His eyebrows rose slightly then he leaned toward her. "It's no dream, sweetheart. Or if it is, I'm having the same one."

He was so close that Victoria could see the subtle shift in his expression, and her breath caught in her lungs. She'd been kissed before, but something told her that sharing a kiss with Trent would be completely different. Because of the friendship they had, they were already closer than she'd been with any of the other guys she'd dated.

"Maybe a kiss would make it seem more real," Trent said, his voice so low that had they been further apart, she might not have heard him.

But she did hear him. "Yes."

And clearly he heard her because he leaned across the last couple inches between them and pressed his lips to hers. Victoria's eyelids fluttered then closed as she felt his hand slip along the side of her neck, his thumb grazing her jawline. And there, with the soundtrack of rain around them, the emotional tendrils that had been reaching out and dancing around each other for so long slowly intertwined and pulled their hearts closer together.

CHAPTER SEVENTEEN

TRENT was gentle and loving in his kiss, and Victoria felt as if every bone in her body had melted when he moved back. He gazed down at her, his eyes a deeper blue than she'd ever seen.

His thumb moved back and forth along her cheek. "You're so beautiful, sweetheart."

The rush of emotion caught Victoria off-guard. That was one word she'd never used to describe herself or heard others use. Her size seemed to bring on descriptions like adorable and cute, but never beautiful. And yet as she looked into Trent's eyes, she didn't doubt that he meant it. That in *his* eyes, she *was* beautiful. It was almost too good to be true.

"Why are you crying?" Trent asked as he swept his thumb beneath her eye.

Victoria gave a choked laugh. She hadn't even realized she was crying. Lifting her free hand, she swiped at the tears on her cheeks. "Emotional overload, I think. I really don't cry often. You've just caught me at some weak moments lately."

"As long as they're happy tears. I never want to be the reason you cry sad ones." He pressed his forehead to hers. "Thank you."

"For what?"

"I know you've had your reservations about me. About us. So I'm thanking you for giving us a chance. You won't regret it, I promise."

Before Victoria could say anything, her phone rang. With a sigh, she moved away from Trent and pulled it from her pocket. "It's my mom."

"Hi, darling. Are you doing okay?" her mom asked when Victoria answered.

"We're doing fine, Mom. We left the park just as it started to rain, and now we're in the driveway waiting for it to stop."

"I'm still out with your dad, but we should be there in a couple of minutes."

"Okay. It looks like the rain is letting up so we might try and make a dash for it."

"You better not be dashing anywhere," her mother scolded.

"No worries, I think Trent will be the only one dashing." Victoria looked over at him and saw him nodding with a grin on his face. "See you in a bit."

"So we're going to make a dash for it?" Trent asked as she slid the phone back into her pocket. "It does look like the rain has let up."

Victoria bit her lip as she stared out the window. "Yeah, I should be able to make it on my crutches now."

"Uh. No. Not gonna take the chance of them slipping on the wet cement. I'm going to carry you." When Victoria looked at him with lifted eyebrows, he added, "You're light as a feather, and it will mean less chance of you injuring yourself this way. Plus, like I said before, I like holding you in my arms."

"Well, in that case..."

Trent gave her a wink before pushing open his door. As she waited for him to come around to her side, she fished her keys out so they'd be ready when they got to the door. There was still a bit of a drizzle, but nothing like the deluge of earlier. She undid her seatbelt as he opened her door.

As he leaned in to slide his arm under her knees and around her back, he pressed a quick kiss to her lips. "Sorry. Couldn't resist."

"You don't hear me complaining, do you?" Victoria said as she leaned her head against his shoulder.

He shut the door with his foot and then moved quickly toward the house. Once they were under the protection of the porch roof, he went to the door and stooped down so she could slide her key into the lock. As the door swung open, he stepped across the threshold and carried her to a chair in the living room.

"I'm going to go get your crutches and wheelchair. I'll be right back."

Victoria nodded and watched as he walked to the front door, still somewhat amazed at what the afternoon had held. But when Trent walked back in with her parents following him, she knew that part of the day was over. She felt a pang of disappointment, and the look Trent gave her seemed to indicate he felt the same way.

"I should probably get going," Trent said as he set her crutches next to her. "Tomorrow is meeting day at work. Always fun."

She moved to grab her crutches, but Trent touched her shoulder.

"Don't get up." He briefly brushed his fingertips across her cheek, his gaze warm. "I'll give you a call."

"Thank you for the time at the park," Victoria said.

His smile was gentle and loving. "Anytime, sweetheart."

She watched him walk to the door, her dad behind him. When her dad came back into the room, he settled beside her mom on the couch and said, "So, anything you want to tell us?"

"Doug," her mom admonished as she patted his knee, but she made no effort to keep the curiosity from her gaze.

"It's okay, Mom." She looked at her parents, hoping that they'd support her relationship with Trent. "Trent and I had a chance to talk this afternoon, and we've decided we'd like to...uh...spend some more time together."

"You're dating," her dad said bluntly, his expression unreadable.

Victoria smiled. "Yeah. We're dating."

Her mom clasped her hands to her chest. "Oh, I'm so happy for you, darling. Trent is a wonderful young man."

"Yes, he is," her dad said gruffly. "I just hope he treats you right."

"He will, Dad. I think he already knows that Eric would come after him if he didn't."

Her dad nodded, a twinkle showing in his eyes now. "It's certainly taken you long enough to figure this all out."

She couldn't argue with him there, but something deep inside told her that now was the perfect time. At least it felt that way to her. Trent, however, might feel differently since he'd waited a long time for her to get on the same page as him.

Over the next few weeks, they fell into a pattern of sorts. Most nights of the week, Trent would come by after work for dinner with her and her parents. Any night that he didn't make it, they would talk at length on the phone before falling asleep.

If the weather was nice, they'd go for a walk around the neighborhood or at the park. She needed her wheelchair less and less as the days passed. By the end of the month after her surgery, it was rare that Victoria used the wheelchair at all. She'd been working hard to strengthen her hip with the exercises the physical therapist had given her to do. It was a relief to finally be free of pain, to not have to fight to hide it from those around her.

On the Saturday before the two-month mark since her surgery, her doorbell rang. Victoria went to open it, pleasantly surprised to see Trent standing there, one hand braced on the door jamb. He wore a black leather jacket in deference to the cooler days now that they'd moved into fall. Under the jacket was a black T-shirt tucked into a pair of tan cargo pants. He looked handsome, but it was the smile on his face that took her breath away.

"This is a surprise. What are you doing here?" When she'd talked to him the night before, Victoria had thought the plan had been for him to go out to the compound for his weekly pounding by Justin. "I thought you were off to shoot and spar."

"I am." He stepped inside and shut the door then bent to give her a lingering kiss. "But I wanted to know if you wanted to come, too."

"Me? I don't know." She did want to go, but the thought of not being able to shoot was depressing. And though she probably *could* get away without her crutches for a bit, she was nervous about doing too much too soon and jeopardizing the progress she'd made so far. It was just one more month until her final appointment with the doctor, and hopefully the green light to leave the crutches behind.

"Well, last night I did a little research. If you're willing to sit in the wheelchair while you shoot, you should be able to do it without taking the chance of straining your hip." He tilted his head, a smile curving up one side of his mouth. "I've missed shooting with you."

Warmth spread through Victoria. Not just because of the smile that she found so attractive, but that he'd thought about her and looked into what would work for her so they could do this together again. She grinned at him. "Sold. Let me go get changed. The wheelchair is in the closet there."

Moving quickly, Victoria went to her room and pulled on a pair of loose jeans, a T-shirt, and a jean jacket. She took a few minutes to brush her hair and add a little bit of makeup. What had started out as a rather quiet and blah Saturday had changed, and she was excited to spend the rest of it with Trent doing something they enjoyed.

When she came out, Trent was standing in her living room staring down at his phone. He must have sensed her presence because he looked up right away.

Sliding the phone into his pocket, he said, "The wheelchair is in the car. You ready to go?"

The walk to the car reminded Victoria of another thing she was looking forward to when she was finally crutch-free—holding hands with Trent as they walked. Though Trent kept a step stool in his car now, he rarely got it out anymore. Usually, he put her crutches in the back and then lifted her onto the front seat. At first, Victoria had protested but when he'd made it clear that he enjoyed doing that for her, she had given up and accepted it. After all, she enjoyed it, too.

And she really appreciated how Trent always picked her up like a lady. Even when she was wearing shorts or pants, he never picked her up under the arms like someone might pick up a kid. He always slid one arm around her back and the other under her knees. And he always buckled her in, sneaking a kiss as he did it.

"I can't tell you how excited I am for this," Victoria said as Trent guided the car onto the highway.

He glanced at her and smiled. "That makes two of us, sweetheart."

As he talked about the research he'd done about shooting from a wheelchair, Victoria realized that aside from her mom and dad, she'd never had anyone spend as much time figuring out how to make things work for her as Trent had. A couple of weeks earlier he'd expressed concern for her safety in his car. After researching he'd taken steps to make sure that she was safely restrained when she traveled with him.

The man made her feel like she was the most cherished thing in his life. It was a totally unexpected feeling. One she really enjoyed. And she tried her best to let him know that he was the most cherished thing in her life, too. At times, it was frustrating because she felt there were far fewer ways for her to show him because he was so totally self-sufficient. Mostly it came down to her cooking and baking for him.

After he had pulled into a parking spot in the lot at the compound, Trent came around and lifted her out and then got her crutches for her. She was relieved that he didn't plan to make her ride in the wheelchair even though she'd need it for shooting.

The last time she'd moved through the hallways of the building, the pain had been almost debilitating. She'd been living on pain killers and a prayer that God would help her to walk without falling since she hadn't wanted to use the crutches around Trent. But then there had come the point where she hadn't had a choice. Thankfully, the end was in sight, and she couldn't wait.

"Good to see you again, Victoria," Justin said when they walked in. The smile he gave her was bigger than any she'd seen on his face before. "Trent told me you'd had some pretty major surgery recently."

"Yes. Hip replacement."

"And your recovery has gone well?" Justin asked.

"Yep. Having lots of physical therapy to strengthen it. I should be free of my crutches in another month or so."

"That is fantastic. I'm sure it hasn't been an easy process." He gave her a warm smile. "You're a strong woman."

Victoria felt a rush of pleasure at his words. "Well, Trent has helped me a lot." She glanced over to find him smiling at her. "And I couldn't believe it when he said it would be possible for me to shoot now."

"When he called me last night to see if I'd approve it, I didn't hesitate," Justin said. "Some of the wounded warriors we work with shoot from wheelchairs. It gives them the feeling of still being able to do something they're good at while they're struggling to come to terms with their situations."

"I never would have thought about it, so I'm glad he did."

"Well, let's get your stuff together so you can get out there."

Trent was aching and sore after his sparring session with Justin but being able to look over and see the smile on Victoria's face helped to ease the pain. He'd been watching something on television the night before when they'd showed someone in a wheelchair shooting. He'd wasted no time contacting Justin to see if it would be possible for Victoria. Clearly, it had been the success he'd hoped it would be. He was just so glad to be able to spend even more time with her doing something she enjoyed, too.

"My part of this deal was to make you a home-cooked meal," Victoria said as he pulled out of the compound a little while later. "But you didn't give me enough advanced warning."

He reached over and took her hand, resting their intertwined fingers on the console between them. "You've cooked me quite a few wonderful meals lately. How about we go out to eat?"

"I'm not really dressed for dinner," Victoria said.

He glanced over to see her frowning. "I'm not suggesting a five-star restaurant. Just someplace comfortable that serves good food."

"Okay."

She still didn't sound entirely at ease with the idea, and Trent wasn't sure why. It wouldn't be the first time they'd been out in public together, although most their recent outings had been limited to the park or the ice cream parlor. In the end, he decided to go to the restaurant that Lucas was part owner of. Victoria had been there before so presumably would be more comfortable in that environment.

When he mentioned it, he could see the tension ease from her and knew he'd guessed right. He still didn't understand her feelings about them being out in public together. Granted, they hadn't gone to places like the mall which would have been crowded with people, but one of these days she would have to face that hurdle and realize it wasn't as big a deal as she thought it would be.

He phoned ahead to see if Amber would save them a table which she readily agreed to do. When they arrived, she took them in immediately. It was barely five o'clock, so the evening rush hadn't started yet.

"Take your time," Amber said after seating them. "Someone will be here to get your drink order in a few minutes."

It didn't escape Trent's notice that Victoria had taken the side of the booth that hid her from the view of most of the rest of the room. Of course, given the training he'd had through BlackThorpe, he would have insisted on taking the side that gave him the best view of the room. Same result but entirely different motivations.

But seeing her relaxed and comfortable, Trent didn't bring it up. There would be time for that later. All he wanted was for her to care less about what the world thought about the two of them being together. If she was okay with it and he was okay with it, that's all that should matter to her. Sometimes he felt that her concerns about how society perceived them were more her imagination than reality. Sure, people stared on occasion, but no one had said anything rude to them. Hopefully with time, she'd become more confident.

They ate their dinner slowly and ended it sharing a wonderfully rich chocolate soufflé.

"I need to get a recipe for this," Victoria said as she dipped her spoon into the bowl. "You're definitely a chocolate lover."

"You betcha, but I'm not the only one. You've matched me bite for bite here."

Victoria laughed, her dark eyes sparkling. "True, but a real gentleman wouldn't have commented on that."

"Ah, well, one slip-up is allowed, right?"

Though he wished they could have stayed there longer, Trent didn't want to tie up the table on such a busy night so he signaled for the waitress to bring their bill. Once he'd taken care of it, they wove their way through the tables to the front of the restaurant and out into the fall air. It was a bit of a crisp evening, but not uncomfortably so.

"Want to walk for a bit?" Trent asked. The restaurant was located on a street with quaint little shops, and he could see other people were taking leisurely strolls along the sidewalks.

Again he saw the apprehension on her face, but he wasn't going to give her a way out unless she outright said no.

"Okay."

As they walked along the sidewalk, he kept his hand on her back. It was the closest thing they could come to physical contact while they walked at this point. "Hey, look. A fudge shop."

"More chocolate?" She looked up at him and grinned.

"Let's go get some."

They took their time picking out a piece of homemade fudge for each of them from the many flavors they had. Trent carried the small bag as they left the shop and continued along the sidewalk. They stopped to look in the windows of a couple of other shops but didn't go inside. As they stood in front of a toy doll display, Trent rubbed his hand on her back, enjoying the feel of her silky hair on his fingers.

"I think Sarah would love this shop. Maybe we'll have to bring her some time," Victoria said as she looked up at him.

His heart clenched at the happiness on her beautiful face. At that point, he would have taken her and Sarah to any doll store in the world they wanted to go to if it made her smile like that. "Yes, we'll bring her sometime and treat her to whatever she wants."

They turned from the store and continued to walk down the block slowly. A group of kids brushed past them, and Trent suddenly had a flashback to the theater. The kids stopped a few yards in front of them and turned around. It was then he realized that they weren't teens but looked to be college age. He braced himself, waiting for one of them to make a comment to Victoria.

"Hey, man!" One of the young men called out. "You into little girls? Is that what turns you on, huh? You're a pervert!"

Rage not unlike what had gripped him at the theater once again flooded him.

"Trent!"

He heard Victoria's voice through the blood pounding in his head but it didn't stop him as he took two quick strides and grabbed a fistful of shirt.

"No, you punk." As he gave the guy a small shake, Trent could see a spark of fear in his light gray eyes. "I'm into that beautiful, courageous and strong *woman* who, though she may be small, has more maturity in her pinky than you have in your whole body. I love her and will not let you degrade her or our relationship by making her into something less than she is. She is *not* a child. She's all woman and yes, she's all mine."

Though he'd spoken the words low, he knew that every member of the group heard him. The ones he didn't have a grip on stepped back. "What is it with you kids these days? Do none of you respect other people and the differences in each of us? You all need to grow up and realize that being different isn't a bad thing. With attitudes like you have, you're all just a pack of bullies."

He let go of the kid and waited for him to scamper away like his friends were doing. Last time, the group at the theater had taken off pretty quickly. This time, the young man stood his ground and met his gaze. "You're right. I'm sorry."

Taken aback by the kid's apology, all Trent could do was nod. The kid spun around and sprinted to catch up with his friends who were now almost half a block away. He stared after them for a moment before turning back to find Victoria. She was leaning against the arm of a bench several yards away, her face pale and her mouth drawn.

It hit him then. This was what she'd been waiting for. This was why she'd been reluctant to be out with him. She'd *known* something like this would happen. And now it had.

"Let's go," he said as he approached her. Though he knew she was likely to protest, he scooped her up and pressed her close against his chest. Her arms were trapped by the crutches, but she held herself stiffly in his arms.

Anger and fear pulsed through him. Would she trust him enough to know that he could handle stuff like this? He didn't care what they said about him. His anger had been because of how it had made their relationship seem, not because of how they'd perceived him. He knew he wasn't any of the things they said. He'd never viewed Victoria as a child and never would.

Once they got to the car, he set her on her feet while he got the keys from his pocket and unlocked the door. She was silent as he lifted her into the car and buckled her in. He usually stole a quick kiss when doing it, but something told him that wouldn't help this situation. Instead, he braced a knee on the bottom of the door frame and leaned back against the dashboard.

He reached out and lifted her chin. Her eyelids swept down, and her eyelashes fanned out against the paleness of her cheeks. "I need you to look at me, sweetheart."

Slowly, her eyes opened and his heart clenched at the pain he saw there. The rage that had ebbed away since the kid's apology returned in a flash. Did those kids even think how their careless words might wound someone? That the thing they chose to tease and mock about was something over which she had no control? That beyond that exterior they chose to focus on was a gentle, loving, beautiful soul?

"It's okay, sweetheart. They were just idiot kids who needed a bit of an education."

She still didn't say anything, but he could see her lips trembling. It scared him to see her like this. There was no way they could live their relationship strictly in safe places away from the crowds of people in the world. Somehow she needed to be able to deal with stuff like this without letting it overwhelm her.

"Please take me home." The words were barely a whisper, and they weren't what Trent had wanted to hear, but he knew they couldn't talk as long as she was feeling vulnerable by being in public like this.

He leaned forward and pressed a kiss to her lips. Soft and gentle, just enough to let her know that he didn't think of her as a child but as a woman.

His woman.

After shutting her door, Trent walked around the back of the car, pausing to take several deep breaths, willing the anger away. Victoria didn't need to see his anger over this.

Unfortunately, she spent the trip back to her house with her head bent, her hands clasped tightly in her lap. What had been such a perfect evening was now threatening to end in a way he just couldn't even consider. Trent wanted to pound the steering wheel but instead kept a tight grip on it as he drove them home.

CHAPTER EIGHTEEN

VICTORIA was relieved when they finally pulled into the driveway of her house. Even knowing the discussion that lay ahead, at least now she was at a safe place.

After turning off the engine, Trent held out his hand. "Your keys."

Victoria fished them out of her purse and dropped them into his palm, being careful not to touch him. His hand hovered there for just a second before he closed his fingers around the keys and got out of the car. He opened the back door and got her crutches and then went to the house.

When he got back, he didn't even give her the option of walking. Trent's jaw was set as he bent into the car to pick her up. He walked with her through the open front door and gently set her down on the couch. Still not saying anything, he walked out of the living room.

Victoria briefly wondered if maybe he was just going to leave. On one hand, that would make it all so much easier, but they'd come so far now that she knew he wouldn't just let it go. He would push about this until it was resolved. One way or another.

She clasped her hands together to stop them from trembling. Though she'd known they were going to face this exact situation, Victoria had never before reacted like she had this time. She had been praying specifically that God would keep them from ever running into someone who would say to Trent exactly what had been said earlier. But they had, and it wouldn't be the last time. She knew that much from experience.

Trent came back into the living room and sat down on the floor in front of her. If he'd settled on the couch beside her, she could have avoided looking at him. But with him sitting right in front of her, Victoria taller than him for a change, it was much harder to not meet his gaze.

"Let's talk about this," Trent said, his expression determined. "What they said tonight didn't surprise you, did it?"

Victoria wondered which response would anger him least, but in the end, she settled for the truth. "No, it didn't."

"You've heard it before?"

She nodded as she looked down at her hands. "You're not the first average-size guy I've dated."

"Look at me, Victoria." The firm request startled her into glancing up and meeting his gaze again. His expression was unreadable, but the gentleness she was used to seeing in his eyes was gone. "Why didn't you tell me? Warn me that comments like that might come our way?"

"I had hoped that they wouldn't." Her voice dropped to a whisper. "I had *prayed* that they wouldn't."

"If you'd told me, I wouldn't have reacted like I did tonight. It took me completely off-guard. I never really thought people would look at us together and peg me as a pervert." Trent's brows drew together. "Was it how I reacted that upset you?"

"Not really." Victoria looked down at her hands again.

"Do you think it's true?" The words were harsh in tone and meaning.

Her gaze jerked up to meet his before she could stop herself. "No. I have never thought that about you."

"Then what is it? Help me understand what's going on here? Why aren't we just brushing this off as comments made by some uninformed idiots and moving on?" He leaned forward, his eyes darkening with intensity. "Why am I getting the feeling that you're going to let this impact us far more than it should?"

And once again it was truth time. Swallowing hard, she said, "I prayed about this. I told God that if He wanted us to be in this relationship, that He had to make sure the ugliness of that accusation would never touch us. But it did."

Trent straightened, his gaze hardening as he stared at her. "So let me get this straight. Because God didn't stop those kids from making that comment to me, this is over between us?"

Was that really what she wanted? Pain shot through her heart. She wanted to have a relationship without the possibility of having it tainted by comments like what they'd heard earlier. She'd wanted to have that with Trent. But now the words had been said. And would be said again.

"Listen, Victoria, we live in a fallen world." Trent sandwiched her clasped hands between his. "God never promised us that things would be easy. Nor that they would be nice. People suffer from far worse accusations and tortures than what I heard tonight. What happened earlier opened my eyes to more of what you've endured because of your size, but it hasn't made me change my mind about how I feel about you. About us."

I'm sorry, Tori, but I just don't think it's going to work. I can't go through life being pegged as a pedophile. It's just not worth it.

She hadn't been worth it. Twice before she'd been through this. And both times she hadn't been worth it.

"Victoria, I don't recognize this side of you." Trent's grip on her hands tightened. "You've always shown yourself to be so strong and confident. Why don't you have enough confidence in me...in us...to know that we can weather something like this? I want this relationship with you more than anything, but I need to know that you want it enough, too. I'm not going to try to talk you into staying with me if you feel like we have to live out our relationship behind closed doors. Sticking only to situations where you feel safe from stuff like what we dealt with today. I refuse to do that. I want the world to know that I'm proud to walk at your side. To hold your hand. To be with you. I need you to feel the same way otherwise it's never going to work."

Trent released his grip on her hands and got to his feet. Victoria looked up at him, dread spiraling through her. Could she do what he wanted? She knew it would be more than just saying she could, he would expect her to *show* him she could.

Fear bubbled to the surface. But what was it a fear of? The fear of having to live the rest of her life without Trent? Or the fear of facing society with its perceptions of their relationship?

Trent cupped her face in his hands and bent down to press a lingering kiss to her lips. When he pulled back, he ran his thumbs over her cheeks. "One more thing you need to know is that I love you. When you're considering what is worth the most in this situation I want you to keep that in mind. Know that I would do all I could to protect you from hurt, but even when I can't—like what happened today—I will love you through those times."

Before Victoria could respond, he turned from her and in three long strides he was out of the living room and into the hallway. Then she heard the door open. Close.

And he was gone.

What have I done?

"What have I done?" Trent muttered the words aloud as he stared out the front windshield, waiting for the red light to turn green.

Giving her an ultimatum like that had to have been the stupidest thing he'd ever done. Opening the door for her to walk out of his life had been stupid. And hard. But it had also been necessary. He needed her to decide to continue their relationship with confidence that it was where she wanted to be. That they would face the world together knowing God would be with them, too.

But it seemed like she had set it up for herself to have an escape. In telling God that if He wanted them together that He would make sure they didn't hear things like they had was setting them up for failure. She knew comments like that were more than likely to come their way. Had she given God a timetable? Because how could she guarantee it would never happen even if they got engaged and then married? Maybe she hadn't wanted this as much as he had.

His heart clenched at the thought, and he thumped the steering wheel with his fist. A horn honked behind him, and he glanced up to see the light had turned green.

Irritated with himself, Victoria and the world in general, Trent didn't check before he pressed down on the accelerator and surged into the intersection. When horns around him blared, he looked to his right to see headlights approaching rapidly as a vehicle ran the red light and plowed straight into him.

Metal crunching.

Tires squealing.

Horns blaring.

Blackness.

Victoria wasn't sure how long she sat there with Trent's words ringing in her head.

One more thing you need to know is that I love you. When you're considering what is worth the most in this situation I want you to keep that in mind. Know that I would do all I could to protect you from hurt, but even when

I can't—like what happened today—I will love you through those times.

He loved her.

And she loved him.

Somehow over the past few months the man who had aggravated her with his lighthearted attempts at flirting had become a friend and then finally, the man who held her heart. But it was that love that was driving her to end things with him. He deserved better than a life with her where he would face accusations—even if they might be rare—that he was a pervert for loving her.

If only she were average size, this wouldn't be an issue for them. She could accept his love the way Staci had accepted Eric's and Brooke had Lucas's.

Victoria grabbed her crutches from the couch where Trent had put them earlier. She slid her arms into the cuffs and gripped the handles. With a sigh, she pushed to her feet and after making sure the front door was locked and the alarm was on, she shut off the lights and made her way to her room.

She paused inside the doorway for a moment then moved to stand in front of the full-length glass mirror doors that covered her closet. She laid the crutches on the carpet and stood still for a moment then her hands went to the button and zipper of her jeans and she stepped out of them. Moving slowly—reluctantly—she pulled off her shirt. Left in nothing but her simple cotton underwear—modest even by swimsuit standards—Victoria forced herself to look at her reflection.

As she stared at her full nearly-naked body in the mirror—something she rarely did—Victoria could only see all the things that were wrong with her. The disproportionate body parts. Though not as noticeable as what other types of dwarfism could have, she was still acutely aware of her longer torso and shorter limbs. Her bottom was slightly heavier and her legs, even with the new hips, still bowed a bit. And now her body had matching scars on each hip.

Ugly.

Beautiful.

So wrong. Like pieces of different bodies stuck together haphazardly.

God formed you in your mother's womb. He does not make mistakes.

Victoria stared at her reflection, meeting her own gaze and seeing the pain there. The mask she put on for everyone else was gone. The mask of strength, confidence, and self-acceptance she'd worked hard to keep in place.

Trent had caught a glimpse behind the mask earlier and then ripped it away with his words. *Victoria, I don't recognize this side of you.*

And now she was trying to face herself without it.

You are fearfully and wonderfully made.

How could she believe that about the body she'd never looked upon with anything but critical eyes, believing it was damaged and flawed? And in her heart she found a small bubble of anger toward God. Why had He given *her* this burden to bear? Why couldn't she have been born the way Eric, Brooke, and Alicia had been? Normal.

What about Sarah? Is she not fearfully and wonderfully made?

That was different.

Victoria shifted her gaze from the mirror as her thoughts went to her niece. When she looked at Sarah, she didn't see the things that made her different from other children. All she saw was a beautiful little girl full of life and love. Would the years ahead hold experiences that would jade her like they had her aunt? Or would she be able to truly accept her differences enough to embrace them and the life God had laid out ahead of her, even if it meant loving a man who might face comments like Trent had tonight?

Victoria knew that in order to be able to have the confidence in their relationship Trent wanted her to have, she needed to have that confidence in herself. In who she was. In who God had made her to be. God hadn't made a mistake when He'd made her. She was exactly the way He wanted her to be. If she was perfectly made in God's eyes, how could she view herself as anything less?

She desperately wanted to look at herself that way. But despite what she'd always portrayed to the world, Victoria knew that if she'd been offered the chance for a "normal" body, she would have taken it in a heartbeat. It was time for her to let that go. She was now—and forever—a little person. It was time to stop letting the fears hold her back from truly living. Truly loving. Not just Trent, but herself.

She reached out to touch her reflection in the mirror and faced the ugly truth she'd been trying so hard to ignore. Deep down, she hadn't been able to really trust in Trent's affection. And as long as she viewed herself as unlovable, she would never be able to trust that Trent really loved her. She'd set up a way out for herself because even though she believed him when he was looking into her eyes and telling her she was beautiful, as soon as he was gone, the doubts ate away at her.

But as she stood there in front of the mirror, Victoria knew that the only love that was in question was the love she had for herself and for God. Trent *did* love her, and he deserved a woman who believed and trusted in his love. She wanted to be that woman for him. For herself.

With slow steps, she moved away from the mirror to her bed. Bracing her elbows on the mattress she covered her face with her hands. Tears flowed as sobs shook her body.

"Please, God, help me to see myself through Your eyes. As something You created with a purpose and not as a mistake. Help me to remember that what You care most about is what is in my heart. I'm sorry for my anger. My fear. Help me to trust You completely with Your plan for my life and with Trent." She paused. "And please don't let it be too late for me with him."

As the emotion ebbed away, Victoria felt more at peace than she had in a long time. And she resolved to counter any negative thoughts about her body and her situation—because she didn't doubt that they would still plague her—with one phrase.

I am fearfully and wonderfully made.

Taking a deep breath, she walked back to where her crutches were and picked them up so she could get ready for bed. Once she was under her covers, leaning back against the pillows, she glanced at her clock. It was nearing midnight. Victoria wasn't sure Trent would still be up, but she wanted to talk to him if he was. Instead of calling, she tapped out a quick text message.

If you're still up, can you give me a call?

Setting the phone on the pillow next to her, she curled on her side, grateful that the soreness of the hip surgery had long since gone. Her go-to sleep position was comfortable once again.

She had anticipated that Trent would call right away. Had he really been able to fall asleep so easily after the emotional upheaval of their evening? Or maybe the drive home had given him time to reconsider what he'd told her. Maybe he— like the two before him—had decided she wasn't worth the hassle.

I am fearfully and wonderfully made.

Minutes ticked by with no call or text. She picked up her phone and swept her thumb across the screen to check the time. It had been almost forty-five minutes since she'd sent the text. He wasn't going to call now.

Closing her eyes, Victoria refused to let the tears fall. If he had changed his mind, she had no one to blame but herself.

When she woke the next morning and found that there was still no return text or call from Trent, Victoria toyed with the idea of going to his church. At one time, he and Eric had attended the same church as she and her parents, but when Eric had switched to attend with Staci, Trent had gone along. Unfortunately, it was a much larger church and had two services, so there was no guarantee if she went that she'd actually be able to find him.

In the end, Victoria went to her regular church, but she had a hard time focusing on the service and breathed a sigh of relief when the pastor dismissed them. She didn't understand why Trent wasn't responding to her text. Surely he would have gotten it by now even if he'd been asleep the night before when she'd sent it.

Back at her house, she changed into a pair of white jeans and a pink shirt made out of a light fabric that was gathered just under her bust and flowed out over her hips. Since she was determined to see Trent that day, Victoria wanted to make sure she looked good. If he didn't call her soon, she was going to go to his apartment.

A little before three, her doorbell rang. Moving as fast as she could on her crutches, Victoria opened her door with a smile of anticipation.

It faltered when she saw Eric standing there. He was still in his church clothes but his tie hung loose and his shirt looked wrinkled. However, it was the expression on his face that had her taking a step backward. Lines of strain bracketed his eyes and his mouth.

"What happened? Are Staci and Sarah okay?" But even as she said the words, she knew he wouldn't be standing on her porch if something were wrong with his family. "Trent?"

"Can I come in?" he asked without responding to her question.

She wanted to slam the door shut and go back to pretending that he was just too busy to call her. Pain pushed past the initial numbness that had come when she'd realized what Eric was there to tell her.

Keeping her head down, she stepped back to let him in. Eric shut the door but didn't move toward the living room until she did. She sank down into an armchair, her hands suddenly too weak to keep their grip on her crutches.

"What happened to Trent? Please don't tell me he's..." She couldn't say the word, just couldn't. She felt warmth on her cheeks as tears fell from her eyes. When she brushed at them, her fingertips felt ice cold on her skin.

CHAPTER NINETEEN

ERIC sat down in the chair next to her and leaned forward. "No. He's not dead."

Relief flooded Victoria but only for a moment before it drained away again. It still had to be serious if Eric was here. "What happened to him?"

"Apparently he was hit by a drunk driver who ran a red light late last night."

"Last night?" No wonder he hadn't responded to her text. He'd been hurt. A sob caught in her throat. "How bad is it?"

"He's pretty banged up. He's been in and out of consciousness. And his right leg is broken. There's some swelling on his brain because he banged his head pretty hard on the side window during the impact. They've ruled out any internal bleeding though."

"Why didn't you tell me sooner?"

"I just found out myself a little while ago. They weren't able to get hold of his parents until early this morning. He had them listed as his emergency contacts. They were in London, but they're on their way back. They called Marcus to let him know and then he called me. We've both been up to the hospital to see him. I wanted to see how he was before I told you what had happened."

"Can I see him?" Victoria felt as if her heart was being shredded with each breath she took. Had she done this to him? Had he been so distracted by their conversation that he hadn't noticed what was coming at him?

"Yes. That's why I'm here. I'll take you to see him. Marcus is there with him right now."

Victoria gathered up her things. Her phone slipped from her shaking hands. She picked it up again, grasping its smooth surface as she slipped it into her purse.

Eric dropped to one knee in front of her and took her hands in his. "Tori. He's going to be okay."

Though fear still filled her, Victoria nodded. "Okay. Let's go."

The trip to the hospital seemed to take forever, but soon Eric pulled into a spot in the parking lot. They walked in silence into the large building, and Eric led the way to the elevator, pushing the button for the fifth floor.

"Marcus made sure he was put in a private room so we can sit with him."

"I thought only family could be with a patient," Victoria said as the elevator doors whooshed open.

Eric stuck a hand out to keep the doors open as she exited the elevator. "Marcus apparently has had some pull as his boss since Trent's family hasn't made it yet. He let them know I was approved to visit, and I asked him to do the same for you. Trent needs you here."

Victoria wasn't too sure Trent would agree, but she couldn't imagine being anywhere else right then.

Eric guided her down the hallway, past the nurses' station to the door of a room. When she hesitated, he looked down at her. "It's going to be okay."

He pushed open the door, and Victoria went ahead of him. She got a quick glimpse of Marcus sitting on the opposite side of the room, but her gaze was drawn to the man lying so still in the hospital bed.

Everything went blurry as she made her way to his side. She blinked and tears fell once again as she saw the bruises on the face of the man she loved. His head had a bandage on it, and his skin was paler than she was used to seeing.

Eric came to stand beside her and managed to lower the railing so she could get closer to him. Victoria reached out and lifted his hand from where it rested on the bed and held it between hers. She pressed it to her cheek, unable to say anything past the tightness in her throat.

"Have the doctors said anything more?" Eric asked.

"No." Marcus's voice was a low rumble. "He came around a little bit ago but didn't say much. Seemed very disoriented still and then fell back asleep. They said he's been that way most the night. Short periods of wakefulness then long stretches of sleeping."

"Tori?" Eric came to where she stood. "Will you be okay here for a bit? Staci isn't feeling well so I need to check on her and, if need be, run Sarah over to Mom and Dad's."

She looked up at him. "Yes. I'll be fine."

"I'll be back in a bit. Marcus will take care of you if you need anything." He bent and gave her a kiss on her cheek. "He's going to be fine. Just keep trusting God."

She nodded. Though Victoria wasn't sure he'd be fine, she was trying her best to trust God for His will in all of this. After Eric had left, it was just her and Marcus in the room. She thought she'd be uncomfortable being alone with the formidable and intense man, but he sat in silence, not offering empty platitudes, and she found that comforting in an odd way.

As her emotions finally settled down, she looked across the bed at him and found him watching her, his expression unreadable.

"Did he seem to be in pain when he woke up?"

"He didn't say he was. He seemed more interested in figuring out where he was and how he'd gotten here. I explained it to him but then he drifted back off again. I'm pretty sure they're giving him stuff for the pain in that." He gestured to the IV hanging above the bed."

"What happened to the other driver?"

Marcus didn't answer immediately but eventually he said, "He was declared dead at the scene. Apparently the impact threw him through the windshield of his truck. He wasn't wearing a seatbelt."

Victoria thought she'd feel glad to hear that the driver who'd hurt Trent was dead, but instead, a sense of sadness swept through her. One bad decision and two lives were impacted. One permanently.

Marcus stood up from his seat and gestured to it. "Why don't you come sit here?"

He pushed the seat right up against the bed and lowered the railing on that side as well. After she sat down, he put her crutches against the arm of the chair. Victoria rested her arm on the mattress beside Trent's, her hand holding his.

"Thank you," she said as she looked up at Marcus.

"You're welcome. I'm going to go down to the cafeteria and grab something to eat. Here's my card. If you need me, just call the number on the back, and I'll come right away."

After he left the room, Victoria drew her legs up and leaned her head against the edge of the mattress in the crook of her arm and closed her eyes and began to pray. She sat that way for about fifteen minutes, but eventually she needed to move around because of the stiffness settling in her hip. She pressed her cheek to his hand, and then slid off the chair, gripping the handles of the crutches as she settled her arms in the cuffs.

As she shifted away from the bed, the door to the room swung open, and an older distinguished couple walked in. Immediately, Victoria knew these were Trent's parents. When she looked at the man, she felt like she was seeing Trent a couple of decades in the future. The woman's gaze swept over Trent and then landed on Victoria.

"You may go. We're here now."

Victoria stared at her. *Go?*

The man cleared his throat. "We're his parents, and we've requested to speak with the doctor in private regarding his situation. I'm sure you have other things that require your attention rather than just sitting here, especially now that we're arrived and can take care of him."

Numbness spread through Victoria. He hadn't told his parents anything about her. And they were just dismissing her as if her presence was meaningless in their world. Not wanting to make a scene in case Trent woke up, she nodded and picked up her purse from the chair. With one last look at Trent, Victoria left the room.

Outside the door, she paused, trying to figure out what to do. Where to go. She had no ride home, but that was inconsequential because she had no intention of leaving the hospital. Trent must have had his reasons for not telling his parents about her, and until he told her that they were definitely through, she was going to be there for him.

"Excuse me," she said as a nurse approached her. "Can you tell me where the waiting room is?"

The sound of muffled voices reached through the sleepy haze Trent found himself wrapped in. He felt as if he were caught in a web and couldn't seem to free himself completely from its tendrils. A couple of times, he'd found the strength to open his eyes, but most the time it was easier to just sink down away from the pain and confusion.

But these voices were insistent and determined. Not to be ignored.

Slowly, he lifted his eyelids. They felt heavy, as if weighted down. He blinked a couple of times at the brightness. Memory flooded back from the last time he'd opened his eyes. Marcus had been there. He'd told him about an accident and that he was in the hospital.

What had happened?

Another memory tugged at him, and he looked down at his left hand. He remembered soft touches. The press of skin to skin.

Victoria?

"Trent! Darling! You're awake." His mother's excited words drew him completely from the fog he'd been in. What were his parents doing there?

"Son, we're so glad you're awake." His dad's expression showed more concern than he'd ever seen from the man before. "How are you feeling?"

"Like I got hit by a truck."

"Considering that's what happened, I'd say you're right on track." Trent turned his head to see Marcus standing in the doorway. The man's gaze swept the room. "Where's Victoria?"

"She was here?" Trent asked. He *had* been right in thinking those touches had been her.

"Yes. I left her with you while I went to get something to eat." Marcus looked at Trent's parents. "Did she say anything to you?"

"Who are you talking about?" his mother asked as she looked from Marcus to Trent.

"My girlfriend, Victoria," Trent said, his impatience clear. "Was she here when you arrived?"

His mother shook her head. "There was just some...girl on crutches. I thought she was a nurse's aide or something."

Trent felt a sick pit form in his stomach. "Mother. That was Victoria."

Her eyes widened in horror as she wrinkled her nose. She leaned toward him and said in a loud whisper, "But she was a...*midget.*"

Anger flared within Trent. How could he expect Victoria to take the world's perceptions in stride when his own family acted like this? "First of all, Mother, don't ever use that term to describe her again. That's derogatory and insulting. She's a little person, and, yes, she is my girlfriend. What did you say to her?"

He saw his mom look at his dad. The older man cleared his throat and lifted his chin. "We just told her she was free to leave as we were here now and needing to speak to the doctor in private."

The anger surging through him burned away the last of the web that had threatened to draw him back into sleep once again. "And she said nothing?"

"No. She just nodded, grabbed her purse and left."

Trent closed his eyes for a moment and when he opened them again, he looked at Marcus. "Can you please call her and make sure she's okay?" He rattled off her cell number as Marcus punched it into his phone.

"I'll find her," Marcus assured him as he stepped from the room.

Though there was a pulsing pain in his head, he kept his eyes open and looked back at his parents. "This is the woman I love. You will treat her as such and never, ever speak to her as anything but the beautiful, caring woman that she is."

"Son, we didn't know," his father said.

"If she was your girlfriend, why didn't she identify herself as such?" his mother asked, her shoulders going back as she stood ramrod straight.

"Probably because she didn't know exactly why I'd chosen not to tell you about her. Although I think she likely has a pretty good idea now."

There was a commotion at the door, but instead of seeing Victoria walk in, Trent stared as his older brother and sister strode into the room, looking for all the world like they owned the place.

"What are you guys doing here?" Trent asked as they came to a stop at the foot of the bed next to his parents.

"Seems your accident called for an impromptu family reunion," his brother said as his sardonic gaze swept Trent from head to toe. "You don't look quite as bad as Mother made your condition out to be on the phone."

"Sorry to have wasted your time, bro. Remind me to change my emergency contact information so they call someone besides you guys next time I'm hurt."

"Trent, don't be that way." His sister came to his side and pressed a kiss to his forehead. "I'm very glad you're okay."

Before she could say anything more, the door opened again. As Tiffany turned and stepped back, Trent caught a glimpse of Victoria as she entered the room. For a moment, she looked like she was going to turn tail and run when she saw the crowd gathered. But then their gazes locked.

Victoria lifted her chin and straightened her shoulders. Without a word to his family, she walked around the foot of the bed and came to a chair that was right next to him. She slid off her crutches as she knelt on the chair and then used the bed to pull herself up so that they were at eye level. With tears sparkling in her brown eyes, she took his hand in hers and held it pressed to her cheek.

"I texted you last night to call me. I guess you didn't get the message."

Trent stared at her for a moment. "Last night? Yeah, I was a little tied up."

Seeming not to care about their audience, she leaned a little closer to him. "I wanted to tell you I was sorry for what happened earlier. For not being strong enough to face the world as us. You were right, and you helped me see that I needed to stop being afraid of what the world thinks about me. About us. And I want you to know that I don't want to live our relationship in only the safe places of our world. I want to live it out where everyone can see that I love you."

A smile spread across Trent's face and the pain in his head receded. He was thankful his arms weren't broken as she leaned closer to press a kiss to his lips. Slipping an arm around her waist, he held her close and said, "You love me?"

"Yes, I do. And I know there're going to be rough times ahead, but I'm going to hold you to your word that you'll love me through them."

"There's no place I'd rather be, sweetheart. When there is love, we can face anything together and come out stronger."

After another kiss, Victoria moved back and finally turned to face his family. Trent nearly laughed at the myriad of expressions on their faces. His mother looked rather shell-shocked, but surprisingly enough, his dad actually looked bemused by the events that had just unfolded before them. His brother's expression seemed to hold a tinge of jealousy. And he really couldn't blame him. Something told him that Todd and his wife weren't nearly as close as he and Victoria were.

"Oh, Trent, this is so romantic!" His sister smiled at Victoria and held out her hand across the bed. "I'm Tiffany. It's nice to meet you."

Since his hand still rested on Victoria's back, he felt the tension ease from her posture, but she didn't move away from him. "And these are my parents, Marina and Everett, and my brother, Todd. Mom and Dad, this is Victoria McKinley, the woman I love."

EPILOGUE

FOUR months later

Victoria stared out the oval window next to her seat. This would be her first time flying, and she wasn't ashamed to admit she was a little worried. Even the opulent interior of Lucas's private jet wasn't doing much to dissuade her nerves. She looked toward the front of the plane where Trent stood talking to Eric and Lucas.

No one else seemed to be suffering any type of fear of flying. Even Danny seemed more excited than frightened. Of course, some of that could be attributed to the fact that he was excited that his mom and Lucas were finally getting married. Though it had been a short engagement by conventional standards, for a ten-year-old boy it must have seemed like an eternity.

"Who are we waiting on?" Lindsay asked as she moved from behind Victoria's seat to where her brother stood.

Victoria saw Lucas and Eric exchange glances before Lucas cleared his throat and said, "Than."

Even from a little ways away, Victoria could see Lindsay's body go ramrod straight. Clearly, she hadn't been privy to her brother's guest list for his intimate wedding to Brooke.

"Than? Why is Than coming with us?" she demanded, her hands on her hips.

Victoria glanced at Trent. As their gazes met, a smile curved his lips and he winked at her. Warmth crept up her cheeks as she smiled back.

"I asked Lucas to invite him."

Victoria looked over her shoulder to see Lincoln making his way to where his siblings stood. Though he still moved with a limp, Lincoln looked a whole lot healthier than he had when she'd first met him at the Hamilton family cabin.

Lindsay swung around to face Lincoln. "Why would you do that?"

The expression on her face was stormy, but Lincoln didn't back away from her. "He's my friend, Linds."

"I know you have some kind of bromance going on with him, but seriously, Lincoln? You had to bring him as your date?" Lindsay's scowl deepened. "Or is he bringing his own date?"

"Now why would I do that when you're already attending?"

Victoria might have laughed at the way Lindsay's expression froze when she heard Than's voice, but something told her that Brooke's soon-to-be sister-in-law wouldn't have appreciated that.

"Nice of you to join us," Lucas said as he held out his hand to shake Than's.

If she hadn't been watching Lindsay, Victoria would have missed the flash of pain on her face before she headed to the back of the plane without even acknowledging Than's presence. She looked at Than and saw his gaze following Lindsay.

What on earth had happened during their date?

Before she could think too much about it, the pilot's voice came over the speakers requesting they take their seats. The nerves that had momentarily left her during the exchange flooded back as she turned to look out the window again.

"You doing okay, sweetheart?"

Victoria looked over to see Trent settle into the seat beside her. He took her hand in his and leaned close to her. "I can't remember...did I tell you how beautiful you look today?"

Warmth again flooded her cheeks as she smiled. "Yes, you did. And you look quite handsome yourself."

"And did I tell you I love you?"

"Yes, you did." She pressed her lips to his. "And I love you, too."

He returned the kiss, his hand lifting to her cheek. "And did I tell you how much I'm looking forward to taking a moonlit walk on the beach with you? Especially now that we're both off our crutches."

Victoria took a quick breath. "I can't wait for that either."

"Okay, you two, break it up."

Trent leaned in to kiss her one more time before settling back into his chair. "Now why would we do that, Than?"

Than had taken the window seat across from them. "Never mind the Love Boat. This is the Love Plane."

"You knew what you were getting into when you agreed to come," Trent said. "Why don't you go sit next to Lindsay. I guarantee there will be no love to worry about there."

Than scowled at Trent. "Just because you've found the woman of your dreams, you don't have to be mean."

"I have found her, haven't I?"

The air in Victoria's lungs whooshed at out that look Trent gave her. She'd never thought she'd be the woman of any man's dreams, let alone someone like Trent. But he was definitely the man of her dreams as well.

The plane lurched and began to move from the terminal. Her grasp on Trent tightened, and he sandwiched her hand between his and rubbed his thumb across the back of her fingers.

Trent knew she'd been nervous about the flight, but he didn't make a big deal out of it. Just gave her his quiet reassurance that it would be okay. As the plane taxied to the runway, she looked out the window at the terminal and planes they were passing. Then the plane swung around and came to a brief stop.

As it began to move forward and gain speed, Victoria braced herself. She'd read that most accidents took place during take-offs or landings.

"Hey, sweetheart."

She turned to look at Trent and immediately felt his lips on hers. As the aircraft broke free of gravity and lifted in the air, Victoria found she wasn't worried about the plane crashing anymore. Because even if it did, being in Trent's arms and feeling his lips on hers would be the best way to go.

"You look beautiful, Brooke," Victoria said as she saw her older sister for the first time in her wedding dress.

Brooke leaned over to give her a hug. "You do, too, Tori. You and Mom did such a beautiful job on that dress."

True to her word, there was nothing poufy or over the top about the dresses Brooke had chosen for the wedding. Her dress was a shade of ivory that complimented her light auburn hair. It had lace straps and a fitted bodice of satin and chiffon that ended in a curved line just below her hips. The chiffon skirt fell to her ankles in the back and was slightly higher in the front. The back of the dress had a corset style lace up that pulled the bodice smoothly over her curves. It was the perfect dress for a wedding on the beach.

Because Victoria was the only bridesmaid, Brooke had let her choose the style and color of her dress. With her mom's help, she had decided on a style and together they'd picked out the fabric and her mom had made it. She'd chosen a soft lilac color, figuring it would be appropriate for a beach wedding and would go nicely with the ivory of Brooke's dress. Choosing the style had taken a little longer, but in the end she'd decided on a fitted bodice with a sweetheart neckline with chiffon straps that tied behind her neck. The bodice ended right below her bust and the skirt fell in soft waves to just above her ankles.

Over the past few months, she and Brooke had had a chance to spend more time together. Though they'd never discussed the things that had pained Victoria's heart, they were closer than they'd ever been, and she was grateful for that. It was a start. A good start.

Victoria lifted a hand to touch the heart-shaped pendant that hung on a white gold chain around her neck. It had been one of the gifts Trent had given her for Christmas along with matching drop earrings. Though she hadn't asked him specifically, she was fairly certain that the stones glistening in both pieces of jewelry were real diamonds. It wouldn't have mattered to her if they weren't, but she had a feeling that Trent would only have given her the real thing.

"We're going to need to go soon," Lindsay said. "We don't want to lose the sun too soon."

"Well, I just want to get married," Brooke said with a grin. "And if I have to do it in the dark, so be it."

Lindsay laughed. "Pretty sure Lucas would agree. I'll just go make sure everyone is ready for you."

She left the room and was back quickly to tell them it was time to go. Victoria followed Lindsay out onto the porch that ran the length of the large house. A breeze sent her dress swirling around her legs as she slowly walked down the steps to the path that would take them to the beach.

"Danny and your dad are waiting just up ahead," Lindsay said to Brooke. "I'm not sure which one is more excited."

As they neared the beach, Victoria heard the soft strains of the string quartet Lucas had flown in for the wedding. The group gathered to witness Lucas and Brooke's marriage was small. Victoria knew them all except for a handful who were acquaintances of the Hamilton family that had arrived shortly after they had the day before.

Taking slow steps, Victoria made her way along the rose-petal-strewn pathway to where the pastor and the guests waited. She looked for Trent. As soon as she found him, their gazes met.

She gave him a shy smile as she neared where he stood. Just before she stepped past him, he mouthed *you're beautiful* and winked at her. Her already warm skin flushed as her smile widened.

Having reached the front, Victoria looked at Lucas and saw that his gaze had gone past her. As she took her spot, she looked from Lucas to where Brooke now approached with Danny on one side and her dad on the other. Victoria wondered if it was at all odd for her given that Lincoln was standing up with Lucas as his best man. The two men stood side by side, but in spite of being twins, they didn't look very similar at that moment. Though they both wore beige pants and light linen shirts, Lincoln had once again grown his hair long so it curled much like Danny's. However, it was the look of love on Lucas's face as Brooke made her way to him that really made them look different.

Once Lucas came to stand with Brooke, her dad took his place next to her mom, but Danny remained with his mom and soon-to-be stepdad.

The pastor spoke briefly then said, "Lucas and Brooke have written their own vows."

"Brooke, when I knocked on your door last year, I had no idea what was in store for us. On so many levels. I had no idea that when that door opened you would be the most beautiful, amazing, loving woman I'd ever met. While my eyes saw your beauty, my heart felt the love you poured into the life of your son. I'm so grateful that you decided to pour that love into my life as well. Each day I wake up knowing that you are in my life is a day that I thank God for. I look forward to what He has for us in the future. I can't wait to love you more each day as we grow closer to each other and to God. I'm here for you. No matter what our future might hold, I will be there for you and for Danny." Lucas turned to the boy who stood next to his mother. "Danny, I can't tell you how proud I am of you and how you've handled everything we faced over the past several months. I know it hasn't always been easy and sometimes it's been confusing, but you have been a champ dealing with it all. I love you, buddy.

Thank you for accepting me into your and your mom's lives. There's no place I'd rather be than with the two of you."

Victoria dabbed at her eyes with the tissue she'd made sure to grab earlier. She knew she wasn't the only one moved by Lucas's words. She was so glad that he had walked into Brooke's life and worked to get past the wall around her heart.

"Lucas, when you appeared on my doorstep, I had already decided that the only guy I needed was Danny. You can imagine my surprise that your arrival in my life had me questioning that. I discovered last summer that my parents had been praying that I would fall in love quickly with the man God had for me. And that's exactly what happened. God knew exactly what I needed and that was you. You stood firm when it would have been easier to step back. You stayed at my side when it would have been easier to walk away. Because of that, I know that together we will be able to face anything. I'm excited to fill our home with the children God sends to us. To see you love them the way you already love Danny. I love you with all my heart and can't wait to spend every single day of the rest of my life with you."

Blinking again at the prick of tears, Victoria looked out at the people standing in the sand and found Trent's gaze on her. There was an intensity in it that she hadn't seen before, and her breath caught in her lungs. She waited for his expression to relax into his usual easygoing smile, but it didn't, and she wished she could read his mind.

When the pastor began to speak again, Victoria turned her attention back to Lucas and Brooke, but her heart was pounding as she kept picturing Trent's expression in her mind. The pastor had them exchange rings and then he pronounced them husband and wife. Everyone clapped as Lucas drew Brooke into his arms and placed a lingering kiss on her lips.

They moved right into taking pictures in order to capture the setting sun before it sank completely beneath the horizon.

"Trent!" Brooke called out. "You and Victoria. No arguments."

Trent held up his hands. "No arguments from me."

Victoria rolled her eyes at Brooke. "Yeah, none from me this time around either."

Once the photographer pointed to where he wanted them, Trent went down on one knee and held out his hand to her. Without hesitation, Victoria took it and allowed him to draw her close to him. She searched his face for the intensity from earlier, but it wasn't there any longer. Maybe she had imagined it.

Victoria positioned herself so that she faced Trent and felt his arm slip around her waist as she rested her hand on his chest. She gave him a shy smile before turning toward the photographer. The photographer quickly got the shots he needed, though Victoria would have happily stood in Trent's embrace if it had taken longer.

What a difference a few months made.

Trent stood on the porch of the small bungalow he was sharing with Lincoln and Than and stared out through towering palm trees at the beach beyond. The sun had set awhile ago, but the moon was nearly full and glistened off the water. Just the previous night, the island had been filled with the sounds of music and laughter as they'd celebrated Brooke and Lucas's wedding. All was quiet now though.

After the small reception had wound down, Lucas had surprised Brooke by whisking her off to another island where they would be spending their honeymoon. From the sounds of things, they were going to be there for a week and then heading to Africa for a couple of weeks.

Listening to their vows during the ceremony had settled something in his heart. The past few months had been trying ones at times for him and Victoria. Once he'd gotten out of the hospital, they'd both had to get around on crutches. They'd certainly made quite the pair whenever they'd gone out. It had limited what they had been able to do, but Trent had been determined that they weren't just going to sit in the house or places that were easy to get to. Once Victoria had said she wanted to live their love out in the world, he hadn't wanted her to change her mind.

Though it had been a challenge, he'd made sure that they made regular trips out into the world. He'd started taking her grocery shopping instead of her mom. At least once a week they would go out to eat, and they'd go to the mall on occasion. After much discussion, they'd made the decision to go to the same church. He'd been willing to go back to the church she attended, but when she said she would go to the church where he and Eric had started attending, he hadn't argued.

They'd gone out to celebrate the day the doctor had told her she didn't need to use the crutches anymore. And then they'd done it again the day he was finally free of his cast and crutches, too. But that night they'd celebrated by walking hand in hand through the mall since it was too cold to walk outside. It was something they'd both been looking forward to. Even now, his favorite thing was to grasp her hand in his as they walked together.

Trent shoved his hands into his pockets and walked down the steps to the lighted path that ran to the main house. He'd said goodnight to Victoria a little while earlier, but he wanted to see her again. Walking slowly, he followed the path to the wide steps that led to the front door of the main house. Light spilled out of the windows and he could hear the sound of voices as he climbed the steps.

He paused in front of the screen door.

"Something on your mind, son?"

At the sound of Doug McKinley's voice, Trent swung around and saw the man sitting with his wife at the far end of the porch. He hadn't seen them initially since they were sitting together without any lights on. Choosing to see it as a sign, he turned from the door and approached the couple.

"Yes, actually there is."

"I thought there might be," Doug said, a hint of laughter in his words.

Had he been that obvious? Well, he supposed everyone knew how he felt about Victoria. Taking a deep breath, he sat down in a wicker chair near them.

He glanced over at the door then said in a voice that he hoped only Doug and Caroline could hear, "I love Victoria very much and with your blessing, I'd like to ask her to marry me."

Doug cleared his throat and leaned forward. "We have prayed for the mates of each of our children over the years, and I'll be honest, we had no idea what that might look like for Victoria. Most of all, we wanted each of them to marry a person who loved God. And for Victoria, we prayed that the man who captured her heart would be a man who would understand her physical challenges and all that might lay ahead for her because of her dwarfism. We've seen changes in her since you came into her life in the role of her boyfriend. She's gained a confidence that we didn't even realize was lacking. She's our baby, and we've been worried about her at times, but I know that I speak for Caroline when I say that we both feel utter confidence in how you will care for our daughter." Doug paused and cleared his throat again. "You most definitely have our blessing, Trent."

"Thank you." He looked at the couple as they sat close together. He was grateful that they had welcomed him into their family not just once but twice. "I will try my best to be everything she needs."

As he stood up, Doug held out his hand. Trent shook it and then bent to hug Caroline. He doubted they would ever know the impact they'd had on his life, and he was so grateful that they were willing to entrust Victoria to his love and care.

"Now let's see what she has to say about it," Trent said as he turned toward the door once again.

When he stepped into the room, he found Alicia, Lindsay and Victoria sitting at a table with tall glasses in front of them. Lindsay's mom was sitting on the couch with a tablet in her hands. She looked up and smiled as he walked in.

"Hey, Trent," Alicia said when she spotted him. "Got bored with the guys?"

"Something like that."

By now Victoria had turned in her chair. "Want to join us? We're just chatting."

Rubbing his fingertips on the soft velvet box in his pocket, he said, "Actually, you up for a walk?"

Her eyes widened briefly before she nodded. "Just let me get my shoes."

Once she disappeared down the hall, Alicia said, "A moonlit walk on the beach?"

"Isn't it required?" Trent tried to keep his tone light. "Would be a shame to come to an island like this and not do it at least once."

Alicia sighed. "Yeah, if you're looking for romance."

Trent looked at Lindsay. "Well, there are a couple other single guys who might be willing to take you on a walk."

Lindsay straightened and gave him a scowl. "I think not." She glanced at Alicia. "But if you're interested, feel free."

Alicia shook her head. "Nope. Not me either."

Trent shrugged. "Can't say I didn't try."

"Try what?" Victoria asked as she joined them again.

"To get them their own moonlit walk on the beach. After all, Than and Lincoln are just sitting in the bungalow talking sports or something." Trent held out his hand to Victoria. "But I'd rather be with my girl. See you guys later."

As they walked out on the porch, he waited for Doug and Caroline to say something, but they remained quiet.

"Wow. I thought it might be too dark for a walk, but that full moon is plenty of light."

Trent had been out earlier in the day to canvas the beach for a place that would be perfect. "I wonder if Lucas and Brooke planned their wedding knowing it would be a full moon on the night they got married."

Victoria laughed. "I wouldn't be surprised at all."

As they reached the sand, Victoria paused. "I want to take my shoes off."

Trent decided that he would as well, because he wasn't going to let her wade in the ocean by herself. Once their shoes were abandoned in the sand, he followed her to the water's edge. "It's great that it's so warm."

"I know. I'm going to hate heading back to winter at the end of the week." She slid her hand back into his as they walked along the shallow part of the water.

Trent found himself struggling to make small talk when there was so much in his heart he wanted to tell her. He wanted to remember every moment of this night.

"Is everything okay?" Victoria asked.

He looked down to find her watching him. "Everything's fine."

"You're just quiet. That's kind of not like you."

In the moonlight, he could see her smile and his heart skipped a beat. "Are you saying I'm a chatterbox?"

"In only the very best way."

They continued to walk along the shore until they reached a large rock that jutted out over the water.

"Let's sit, sweetheart," Trent suggested.

She looked at the rock and then said, "You're going to have to give me a hand up."

"Never a hardship," Trent said with a grin as he scooped her into his arms. Before he placed her on the rock, he bent to kiss her. Her arms went around his neck and held him close to prolong the kiss.

Even though he didn't want to end it, he moved back a bit and set her on the rock. She moved over so he could climb up beside her and then snuggled into his side as he put his arm around her.

Holding Victoria close, Trent remembered their first kiss. That change in their relationship had been set to the soundtrack of water as they'd sat in his car in the midst of a rainstorm. And now, hopefully, their relationship would change once again as they were surrounded by the sound of the waves as they rushed the shore and then swept back.

The breeze off the water was cooler than Victoria had thought it would be, and she wished she'd brought a jacket.

"Cold?" Trent asked when she snuggled closer to him.

"A little. I guess once the sun goes down, the temperature drops, too."

He ran his hand up and down her arm. "Want to go back?"

She glanced up at him and shook her head. "I just need to remember what cold really is. This is nothing."

As he stared down at her, she felt his hand brush against her cheek. Warmth from his touch swept through her, chasing away the chill of the night air.

"Do you remember that day in the park?"

"I'll never forget that." She smiled. "Or sitting in your car in the rainstorm afterward."

"My personal favorite moment was that day in the hospital."

Victoria felt a tendril of excitement wind its way through her. "When I told you I loved you?"

"Yes. My body may have been banged up pretty good, but you filled my heart that day and chased away the pain."

Victoria turned toward him, pressing her cheek to his chest and drawing her legs up to rest them against his thigh. "Worst and best day of my life all wrapped into one. I was so scared I'd lost you."

"You're not going to be able to get rid of me that easily," Trent said with a chuckle that she felt as much as heard.

"Then I guess it's a good thing I don't want to get rid of you." Victoria felt his arm tighten around her.

"I don't want that either. Ever." He shifted slightly and then she felt his fingers under her chin, tilting her head up. "I can't imagine what my life would have been like without you.

I had a small taste of it, and I could hardly bear the pain." His thumb brushed against her cheek. "But I want more. I want to start each day looking at your beautiful face and end it with you in my arms."

Victoria's heart skipped a beat and then began to pound even harder. She started to say something, but he pressed his thumb lightly against her lips.

"I want to be there when you need me—night or day. I want to know that you're also there for me—night or day. I want to share whispered dreams and words of love in the darkest of nights. I want you in my life forever."

His hand moved from her face and when Victoria looked down, she saw a sparkle in the moonlight. She could hardly breathe as a band tightened around her chest.

"I love you, Victoria McKinley. Would you please marry me and spend the rest of your life as my wife?"

Tears spilled over as she turned and wrapped her arms around him, burying her face in his chest. She had hoped and prayed that this moment would happen. She'd had no idea he'd been planning this, but it was so perfect. So romantic. And all for her.

She lifted her head and looked into his eyes. "I love you, Trent. And yes, I would love to marry you and be your wife. You're everything I never knew I needed in my life. You've made me stronger and helped me find joy in the things that are important. I can't imagine living the rest of my life with anyone but you."

As his head lowered, Victoria whispered a prayer of thanks. The touch of his lips to hers filled her with wonder that this amazing man was going to be hers. She knew that she could trust him, lean on his strength, and that together they would be able to face everything that was to come because of the love God had given them for each other.

The End

OTHER TITLES BY

Kimberly Rae Jordan

Marrying Kate

Faith, Hope & Love

Waiting for Rachel (*Those Karlsson Boys: 1*)
Worth the Wait (*Those Karlsson Boys: 2*)
The Waiting Heart (*Those Karlsson Boys: 3*)

Home Is Where the Heart Is (*Home to Collingsworth: 1*)
Home Away From Home (*Home to Collingsworth: 2*)
Love Makes a House a Home (*Home to Collingsworth: 3*)
The Long Road Home (*Home to Collingsworth: 4*)
Her Heart, His Home (*Home to Collingsworth: 5*)
Coming Home (*Home to Collingsworth: 6*)

This Time With Love (*The McKinleys: 1*)
Forever My Love (*The McKinleys: 2*)
When There is Love (*The McKinleys: 3*)

A Little Bit of Love:
A Collection of Christian Romance Short Stories

For news on new releases and sales
ign up for Kimberly's newsletter

http://eepurl.com/WFhYr

Please visit Kimberly Rae Jordan on the web!
Website: www.kimberlyraejordan.com
Facebook: www.facebook.com/AuthorKimberlyRaeJordan
Twitter: twitter.com/KimberlyR Jordan

Made in the USA
Monee, IL
02 January 2022

87675402R00125